ALGONQUIN

Cort Fernald

Thanks to Russ Hunt for proofreading ALGONQUIN.
Thanks cannot adequately express my gratitude to S.H. for advice and the tireless effort on the format and cover of ALGONQUIN.

Algonquin/ Cort Fernald. -- 1st edition
ISBN-13: 978-0615832180
ISBN-10: 0615832180

For family and friends...

{-1-}

"Tobys dying"

With a buzz, the text popped on Royce's phone as he closed the door of the cab.

He missed a step, murmured "wha?" and staggered across the sidewalk. Royce braced himself against the brick doorway of Riggins Sport Apparel warehouse. He had a few minutes before his meeting with old man Riggins.

The text was from Frank Lofstrom, Royce's boyhood friend. He always had to be the first in news. Frank was the only one of Royce's pals he had stayed in contact with over the years.

Royce shouldered his laptop and turned so the sun didn't reflect off the phone.

"What from? Hospital?" he typed, using his thumbs.

"Sherman Hosp Elgin Il..." was the quick reply. "Its Cancer! U in CA? U in US?"

"Yes NYC," Royce typed back. "Im going...U?" It was a snap decision.

He had to get to his meeting with Riggins. He slipped his phone into the inside pocket of his suit jacket and went into the warehouse. It was all noise and chaos of beeping fork lifts loading trucks across the warehouse floor as Royce climbed the iron stairs to the second floor offices. He knocked on the loose glass of the door to Riggins' office. The old man behind the cluttered desk glanced up and motioned Royce to come in.

"Partridge," he growled, chewing the stub end of an unlit cigar stuck sideways in the corner of his mouth. "It's about goddamn time!" He waved at an old leather covered chair in front of the desk. There was a rip down the middle, with yellow stuffing coming out.

"Traffic," Royce said, putting his laptop on the floor and taking a seat. "Good to see you again, Mr. Riggins."

"Yeah, cut the crap," he barked. "I'm busy...let's get to work."

Royce's phone buzzed.

"What the hell is that noise?" Riggins asked, his bushy grey and black eyebrows low.

"Just my phone," Royce assured him, opening his laptop bag, pulling out a batch of four-color pages. "Here are the updated proofs."

"Well, turn the god damn thing off," Riggins said, taking the stack of proofs with both hands and over his desk. "I ain't paying for you to talk on the phone."

Royce sat back while Riggins started leafing through the proofs. He must be in his eighties, Royce thought. It could only have been his orneriness that kept him going. Royce didn't think much of Martin as an art director, in fact he thought he was a prick, but he was right about personally meeting with Riggins. The old man had been getting a pitch from another graphics company. Royce had been in and out of Riggins non-air conditioned Brooklyn warehouse office for two days--two sweltering summer days in New York. He patiently sat, stuck to the leather chair while the old man, in rolled shirt sleeves and wet arm pits, literally poured over page after page of proofs questioning fonts, headers, graphics and layout. Royce, finding the office almost unbearably close, took his time answering every grunt and wheeze on why this photo choice and type style was selected for Riggins Sport Apparel's winter catalogue. It was worth the discomfort. Riggins was the largest and most lucrative account the firm had and Royce treated him as if he was their only client.

"I know you birds," Riggins said chomping his cigar. "You say we could do this E-ah-lectronically." His wild eye brows jumped up and then down as he squinted across the paper strewn desk. "I'm a dinosaur, an old jew brontosaurous-stein and I'm paying you San Francisco whiz kids buckets of money each and every year to put out our Christmas book. That's our moneymaker. Sure, we could use those twatter things and that email stuff—but I want someone here...here to answer my questions now." Riggins scowled at Royce a moment. "I want a face to look at...not some TV."

Royce wiped the sweat trickling down his temples and wholeheartedly agreed. He wasn't just one of the firm's best accounts, this was Royce's annual bonus. Still, he couldn't stop himself from asking Riggins, "Have you given any thought to upgrading your website with the links I suggested?"

The old man grumbled something that sounded like an affirmative and that was as far as it went. Royce made a mental note to add the link regardless, knowing the increased hits and click-throughs would push his online sales.

After a sweltering hour watching Riggins flip and grunt through all the pages, the old man changed very little. He scrawled an OK and his initials and handed the stack back to Royce. They shook wet palms and Royce stuffed the proofs back in his laptop bag and left.

Down the street from Riggins Sports warehouse was a soot stained red brick Catholic church. Royce pulled open the heavy wooden door and stepped inside. It was dark, with thick stale air faintly smelling of incense. He felt his way to a far corner pew and sat. He was among shadows and breathed in the coolness of the air. Yet, it comforted him. The stained glass window was cracked and dirty grey. Occasionally, a hunched figure would cough. Small white men in starched black robes busied themselves laying out golden goblets and multicolored silk sashes upon a clothed alter. "The house of regret," Royce thought. He pulled out his phone and opened the text message. "Cancer," Royce thought. "What the hell is going on with Toby?" There was another text from Frank. In the iridescent green glow of the screen Royce read: "Saw him today...just leaving...hes bad...hurry."

Hurry? Royce thought, staring up at the brightly lit crucifix above the pulpit. It was so theatrical; a benign and kindly Jesus in calm repose and garish stage makeup, head tilted to the side with imploring eyes cast upward. He thought of the brutally tortured Jesus in small, out-of-the-way Mexican roadside churches he had seen down in Oaxaca. That Jesus, with thick rivulets of crimson blood from the deep pricks in the crown of thorns trailing down his drawn and agonized face, seemed more real to him now.

Life is like a prayer, he thought, whispered excitedly and full of wonder when young; spoken firm and froth with demands when mature; sadly murmured with regret until a final amen.

"Wheres Will?" Royce typed back to Frank, rising from the pew. He had to check out of the hotel and get to the airport for his afternoon flight.

He left the church, stuffing a couple of dollars into the poor box on the way out. "For Toby," he whispered.

Martin was rude as usual when Royce phoned him as he rode the shuttle to Newark airport.

"Riggins okayed everything," Royce told him. "He made a couple of changes to the text on the ladies workout clothing. Not much else. I'll scan and send to Jennie to reset."

"Yeah, I knew he would," Martin said, with a very pleased tone to his voice. "When are you getting back to the office?"

Royce took a breath. This might be a fight. "I've got an emergency, so I won't be back in until Monday."

"Emergency? Monday?" Martin said, his voice rising. "What kind of emergency?"

"It's a family emergency." He lied, knowing Martin would have objected had he known why. "I have to stopover in Chicago for a couple of days for a family emergency. I'll take accrued time," Royce added.

"Damn right you will," he snapped back. "Just get back in on Monday...early!" And he abruptly hung up.

It cost Royce an extra $200 to change his Newark to Chicago to San Francisco flight from a three-hour to a two-day layover in Chicago. He knew he would have a battle with Martin expensing this leg of his trip since he was taking the two days. He was through security and had a long wait in the terminal until the flight started boarding. There was a gate with no flights scheduled and Royce took one of the empty seats and opened his laptop. He did an online search for hotels in the northern Illinois area. He wanted to find a hotel near Algonquin, his hometown. There was a Holiday Inn Express in Crystal Lake; a Marriott in Barrington. He checked rates and availability, he was cutting it pretty close, and both hotels were booked.

His phone buzzed. Royce picked it up and looked. It was a text from Frank.

"Will???? Dont know," he replied to Royce's previous text.

"Later" He typed and sent.

Scrolling down the page Royce saw Algonquin Guest House. It was a B&B and in town. He went to the website and checked availability. They had a vacancy for tonight and tomorrow. Royce filled out the information and put in his credit card number and sent. "That was lucky," he thought. He had not been in Algonquin in more than forty years. This was a sad occasion for sure, but he was interested to see his hometown after so long.

"Shit," he said quietly, he had almost forgotten to call Jessica and let her know he would be staying over in Algonquin.

He called and got voicemail. After the beep he said, "Hey, Jess...I am not coming in tonight. I am stopping off in Chicago for a couple days. I'll call later tonight. Hope you and the cats are okay. Miss ya." Royce clicked off.

Boarding was announced for Royce's flight to Chicago. He stowed his carry-on in the overhead bin and settled into his aisle seat in business class. It didn't look to be an overcrowded flight and as always, Royce hoped no one took the window seat so he could put up the arm rests and stretch out. He opened a book and pretended to read as passengers filtered down the aisle and found their seats.

"Excuse me," an effeminate man in a blue suit said to Royce. He looked up. The man pointed to the window seat. Royce stood and stepped aside as the man slipped past to the seat. He glanced back and smiled. Royce ignored it and sat back down, opening his book.

"Going to Chicago on business?" the man inquired in a friendly manner. "Or pleasure?"

"Neither," Royce replied. "An old friend is in hospital, dying."

"Oh oh," the man breathed, his hands to his face and looking embarrassed for his faux pas. "I'm so sorry."

"It's alright." Royce said quietly, holding up his book, a signal ending the conversation.

The cabin door was shut and secured and the crew made ready for takeoff. Royce absentmindedly watched the flight attendant demonstrate how to click the seat belt and where the exits were located. The taxi out and takeoff was routine and they were soon at cruising altitude.

Royce couldn't concentrate on reading, thinking about Toby. Toby had been his best friend: the guy most kids wished they were, not just because girls were attracted to him. He was well-liked, with Nordic good looks, funny and had an engaging smile with rows of perfect teeth. Toby would flash a smile and there was no way you could resist returning a smile. Then there was Will, a big, genial kid, with a ready laugh. However, just below the surface, Will had a streak of quick anger. He was terribly self-conscious about his bad complexion. That was unspoken. But, if you were in a fix and needed a friend, Will was there for you. And Frank cautious, quiet, obedient to mom and dad and someone who prided himself on never having missed a single homework assignment in school. That boast always met with gibes and jeers from the others. Frank's one character trait was that he would complain, early and often. Royce and Toby were alike in many ways and had become fast friends. Looking back Royce realized his troubled home life and rebelliousness were things Toby admired. Sometimes Toby would defer to Royce; which he didn't understand at first, because Toby never stepped down to anyone. But Royce came to realize that for all his leadership and ready personality, Toby lacked self-confidence. If things went wrong he would retreat into a shell. It took awhile to get him coaxed out of the shell. But these were the times when Royce stepped forward. The four were like the corners of a square, Toby and Royce the top corners, with Will and Frank supporting them at the bottom.

The drinks cart dragged down the aisle and Royce asked for a soft drink and small snack. The flight wasn't too long, but it was tedious. The constant drone of the engines lulled Royce into a half-sleep. His thoughts drifted back to the last time he saw Toby.

Crowds swelled Grant Park as the summer evening came down easy and the city lights shined. Speakers with handheld megaphones stood on a makeshift stage and exhorted the mob with anti-war speeches, civil rights, free so and so. Royce didn't understand all the rhetoric. A cool breeze came in off Lake Michigan making the sound of revolution waver over the air. But there was tension and it was electric. You could see it in darting eyes and fearful expressions because surrounding the park were double lines of Chicago police, in riot helmets and armed with mace and long black truncheons. Lines of black paddy wagons were parked behind the blue shirted police.

"Hell no, we won't go."

"Stop the war."

A few city blocks away, at the International Amphitheatre, the Democrats were nominating a candidate for president.

Royce was there at the urging of Denny and Rob, two musician friends. "There'll be tons of chicks, man," Rob said.

Looking around Royce saw Denny and Rob smoking with a group of girls sitting in a circle, passing around a gallon jug of red wine. The girls were smartly dressed, with page boy hairdos. Royce pegged them for co-eds from Northwestern. One had a large white McCarthy button pinned on her sweater. "Clean for 'Gene'" thought Royce.

The crowd was a mix of 18-30 year olds, hippies, clean-cut pipe smoking intellectual types, even some leather-clad greasers all mingling expectantly in the park. Waving signs and peace flags popped up here and there above the painted faces and pig masked masses. The cops were active, squad cars going back and forth, with more cops joining the police line. At the urging of a speaker the crowd started to move out of the park, into the street, marching to the convention hall. All around him people started to move and Royce was swept along.

"Hey! Hey! LBJ...how many babies did you kill today..."

The police line parted and let the demonstrators through. Up the street they marched. It seemed a peaceful protest.

But then a brick went through a store window. Screams came from the back of the crowd as police, flailing their batons, charged into the marchers. Rocks and bottles started flying toward the police.

And they ran.

"Walk!" someone shouted.

"You walk," another yelled pushing by Royce.

A blue line of cops waded into the people, swinging truncheons like machetes cutting through the jungle. Royce ran down the middle of the street. Store windows were smashed up and down the street. The glass glistened like crystal in the street light.

Tear gas clouds billowed above the crowd. The air became sharp and choking with each breath.

The cops had let half the demonstrators leave the park and then closed the line and cut off the rest.

People were dodging left and right, trying to get away. Royce glanced back. The cops were getting closer. He stumbled against a parked car and looked back to see a girl pinned against a station wagon being beaten over and over by a cop. A boy went to grab the cop's truncheon, only to have another cop come up and knock him cold to the pavement with one blow. They dragged the unconscious boy and bloody girl back to a paddy wagon.

Royce ran with the crowd as it turned a street corner. The gas was stinging his eyes. People were shoving and pushing; some fell and were trampled.

"Walk."

The crowd surged up a side street to an old grey steel girder railroad bridge over a canal. There they were stopped cold by a line of National Guard troops. Searchlight beams flicked across the dark sky, casting eerie shadows and light on the bridge and building faces. The guardsmen wore gas masks, with helmets and M-14s crossed. Bayonets gleamed in the stray light. The guardsmen's line sagged with the crush of protesters. But they pushed the crowd back.

"Let us through," people yelled.

"They're beating us."

The guardsmen held the line.

"Here they come," someone cried.

Scattered groups of police were beating their way through the protesters, trapping demonstrators between them at the railroad bridge.

Sirens tore through the night.

A girl tried to leap over the line of guardsmen, but was caught in midair and hurled back.

Protesters were throwing punches at the guardsmen. A rifle butt in the chest staggered one. Royce had his hands on a guardsman's rifle and was wrestling him back. He caught a glimpse of the guardsman's eyes behind the black rubber gas mask. He was Royce's age and looked terrified.

Tear gas canisters popped and blue clouds burst, blinding people. They coughed and gagged.

"Royce!"

Someone called his name. Startled, Royce frantically looked around.

"Royce!"

It was a guardsman down the line pushing back protesters, looking aside at Royce. Through burning tears Royce could make out the eyes in the gas mask.

"Toby?"

"Fuck yeah! Get over here..." the muffled voice yelled.

Royce fought his way over to Toby. A tall shirtless man with wild red hair and red beard was throwing punches at Toby, screaming he was going to kill him. Royce pushed the redhead away. Suddenly Royce was staggered by a glancing blow to the side of his head. Angrily, he turned thinking it was the redhead. But a cop had the redhead by the hair and was dragging him backward. A second cop, with raging eyes behind his Plexiglas face mask, was winding up his truncheon to it bring down again on Royce.

Toby grabbed Royce by the collar of his blue jean jacket and dragged him through the guardsmen's line. He fell on gravel between railroad tracks, choking with stinging tears streaming down his face, his head throbbing. He struggled up. Royce looked back at Toby shoulder to shoulder with other guardsmen, holding the line.

Olive drab National Guard trucks were angled on the other side of the bridge, blocking it. A small group of guardsmen stood by the trucks, smoking. They saw Royce limping toward them.

"Just keep going, kid. Get the hell out of here." They motioned him to move on.

Royce sunk down on the curb.

"Don't say we didn't warn ya."

The cops had pulled most of the protesters off the line of guardsmen and those that couldn't escape were clubbed or taken away under arrest. Noise raged throughout the city, with sirens and the low rumble of masses of people moving down the streets. "Pigs are whores" someone shouted in the distance.

The guardsmen along the bridge tightened their line. Royce wiped the tears from his eyes with his shirt. He touched his head. There was a knot the size of an egg. He looked at his fingers—there was a smear of blood across his fingertips.

"What the fuck are you doing here?"

Royce glanced up. It was Toby. He had his helmet and gas mask in his hand, his M-14 rifle butt cocked on his hip.

"Man, am I glad to see you," Royce said. "Thanks."

"You're not one of those Yippee guys, are you?" Toby asked.

"No," Royce shook his head. "I was with Denny and Rob. They thought they could meet some chicks."

"Chicks?" Toby let loose a laugh. "This is a fucking war zone. Hey, check this out." He jerked back the bolt of his rifle and out tumbled a shiny brass round, spinning through the air and tinkling onto the gravel. Royce picked it up and turned it in the light. It was a brass jacketed live round.

"That's what they issued us." Toby said.

"You really like this shit, don't you," Royce said.

"Dammit," Toby beamed. "I do. I really do."

{-2-}

"We are making our descent into Chicago..." the pilot said over the cabin's speakers.

It was strange returning to the place where, in his heart, he had never really left.

Royce had flown in and out of O'Hare International since it was first opened. An experienced traveler he was off the plane with his laptop and carry-on, on the moving sidewalks and down to the lower level and out to the rental car companies shuttle buses and at the rental counter in less than half an hour.

A 747 roared just overhead, ripping through the slate grey sky. Royce ducked from reflex, though he was in no danger from the jetliner coming in low over the 190 link to the Tri-State toll way out of O'Hare International. He smiled, glancing aside at the big bird's gleaming white underbelly passing overhead, with landing gear down, lit flash by flash from the strobes marking the runway approach.

Headlights came quickly into his rearview mirror, and Royce realized he'd let off the accelerator when the jetliner gave him a start. The heavy, gadget-laden mid-sized rental coupe automatically downshifted with a lurch. Amber and green digital displays on the dash rivaled the neon of Broadway Street at home in San Francisco. He fiddled with what he thought was the air conditioning, but was hit with a blast of hot air. He didn't need that on the hot and humid August evening. Pressing other buttons Royce managed to turn the heat off, but somehow activated the passenger seat so it tilted back like an upset rocking chair, then locked and unlocked and locked again all car doors.

After a number of sharp banking turns to the left and merging into traffic, Royce was heading out of Des Plaines and on the toll way north.

He came to see Toby, but thought, you can't go home again. And throughout his flight from Newark he wondered just what the hell he was doing. Home? It'd been nearly forty years since he'd left Illinois. It really wasn't home. His sister had fled to college, then fled into a marriage, then had children to care for, and a divorce and years of therapy and never returned. His parents had divorced as soon as they'd got him out of the house. He was the last child gone and there wasn't enough booze in the known world to keep them together, when they had lived to despise each other for so long. His father had remarried long ago, moved to Florida (where they didn't make you pay alimony) and died of cancer years ago. It was a death like his life, full of fear and anger, thinking people were out to get him. Royce visited his bedside, a dutiful son silent and standing dispassionately away from the man he despised. He stood just beyond arm's reach. Royce's mother had returned to her native New England. She'd got sand in her shoes (as she liked to say) and lived happily on Cape Cod until cancer took her as well. But Royce remembered her sitting on her porch watching ominous grey and blue/black clouds of a nor'easter brewing-up over the Atlantic, with an unfiltered smoke in one hand while drinking that horrible concoction of orange juice and whiskey she so loved in the other. He was there to see Toby because there was nothing like a family home. But it was a special place to revisit; a poignant time in his life to recall. It was where Royce had spent his formative teenage years. Not so much home, as the home of his most enduring memories, the painful and happy times.

He drove through the gathering dusk, easing up to the toll booth and handing the toll taker in the booth a five dollar bill, cupped the change and drove off. In the long reach of the headlights the toll way stretched deep into the dark, flat land. Royce left the creeping bright of Chicago behind and was now in the far northern suburbs. Every now and again exits curved into large clusters of houses and streetlights, car lights and stoplights. He cruised by Elk Grove Village, Arlington Heights. Passing through Hoffman Estates he knew he was getting close to Elgin and the Highway 25 exit. It was all too familiar—like he was 18 again and driving home in the early morning hours after being with a co-ed in Evanston.

Forty years ago these were small, isolated villages, separated by large expanses of farm or vacant land. Now it seemed as if it was one huge sprawling suburb with little open space between Elk Grove Village and Hoffman Estates. Royce wasn't surprised, fully expecting it to be built-up. Though, it made him wonder about the changes to the little town of Algonquin on the Fox River. Sure, it'd be different, but how much had it changed since he left high school? Though most of all the Fox River; he wouldn't be able to bear it if he didn't recognize the river he and his buddies had spent so many summers on.

There was his exit.

Royce flipped on the turn signal and was startled by windshield wipers. "Dammit, I'll never figure this car out," he murmured to himself as he exited the toll way.

The Dundee, Carpentersville area had become a vast expanse of tract homes, a strip mall here, convenience store and fast food restaurant there. Carpentersville, a lower middleclass suburb, always had the potential to be urban blight. It'd been carved out of a cornfield after World War Two and developers, like nature itself, abhorred open land. Along with more houses, there were stoplights at nearly every intersection.

This stretch of Highway 25 was the strip they used to cruise every weekend—from McDonald's down through the Meadowdale Shopping Center and back again. A dollar's worth of gas went a long way in those days. Round and round and round with Toby, Will and Frank, whiling away sultry summer evenings, either straight, sometimes drunk, occasionally stoned, with the radio blasting Summer in the City or the latest Beatles tune. But for the most part, they were on the look out for girls. "Hey, babe? Wanna ride with us? C'mon, honey!" Yeah, that always worked, he bemusedly thought.

At a stoplight Royce glanced over to the car in the next lane. The jacked-up dirty white and grey primer splotched sedan was full of teenagers bouncing and laughing to the steady bass thump of hip hop. The long hair, the short hair, crooked caps, there was little to distinguish this crew of cruising kids from the cruisers in Royce's day. He thought that these could be the kids of people that went to high school with him. But after forty years they just may be their grandkids. Smoke curled out of the passenger side window. They squealed off at the first flash of green light. Royce had to smile, impatience is the providence of youth, and gently pressed the accelerator.

As they sped off he couldn't help but think of Toby, Will, Frank, Denny and Rob—along with scores of old buddies. Other than Frank, Royce had lost touch with them. He'd left without a trace, left on purpose. He hated the idea that any of those guys might now be fat, balding and delivering pizzas. Luckily, no twenty, thirty or forty year high school reunions had found him. But now Toby was dying. It made him sad.

He drove by a corner he recognized and remembered a girl that used to live on that street.

"Oh, what was her name?" He asked himself aloud, recalling her face but not her name. For an instant he had the urge to turn around and drive down the street and find her house. What would he find? Not the girl from long ago. Thinking of Stephanie (yes, that was her name), he let out a sigh, unconsciously twirling the gold band on his left hand with his thumb.

The bright lights of Carpentersville faded as he dipped over a hill toward the junction with Route 62.

It used to be a solitary stop sign set in a crossroads that branched out like crow's feet, surrounded by cow pasture and cornfield. Now, the junction of Highway 25 and Route 62 was a major intersection, with cars whizzing by convenience stores and gas stations, a restaurant, bowling alley and auto dealership. The large green sign had big arrows pointing to the right and snooty suburb of Barrington; and Algonquin to the left. Cars were going in all directions and in a big hurry. Royce waited for the arrow and turned left. He drove down 62, past memories all along the road. He worked graveyard shift at a gas station over there. He'd prop the chair against the door and sleep through the dead hours 3 o'clock till dawn. The night he was robbed at gun point came back to him. He couldn't give those guys the money fast enough. The gas station was gone. There was a driving range and batting cage somewhere along 62. And a gravel pit was over the hill. In the darkness he saw the driving range was also gone, but the gravel pit was still there. Driving ranges and gas stations become apartment complexes, furniture stores and auto wrecking yards; but gravel pits are forever.

The closer he got to Algonquin the less Royce saw drastically changed. More houses built in a field at the crest of the Fox River Valley, and yet across 62, discernible in the headlights a line of rusted barbed wire fence skirting a cornfield with tall late summer stalks about ready for the combine.

On the left was a street leading to his old school, Algonquin Junior High.

There was the baseball diamond and field they played football on.

In a flash he saw a rectangular green sign: ALGONQUIN pop. 30,000.

Wow, he thought, there were only about fifteen hundred people when we moved here.

He glided down the gently sloping valley toward town. Nothing seemed startlingly different as he slowed to 30 miles an hour and neared the wide concrete bridge over the Fox River. He glanced to the right, passing River Road. How many times had he taken that turn toward home? Even then, after so many years, he still had an impulse to turn left on River Road, down about a quarter mile and up Wood Street. The road wasn't well lit. He'd go down it in daylight tomorrow.

Over the bridge he caught sight of the dark width of the river along the valley floor. There were no lights from boats on the river, but single lights shown from piers and houses along the banks. And with a bump off the bridge, he was under the lights of Algonquin. It still has a bump, Royce thought bemusedly.

Route 62 ended right in the center of Algonquin. Amazed, Royce saw the town was almost unchanged. After all this time it was familiar and eerie. Of course, nothing was actually the same, more stores and neon, yet he had a funny feeling, as if he were a kid riding his bike into town for a soda instead of an older man driving a rented car he didn't understand.

Route 31 crossed Algonquin and for a couple of blocks masqueraded as Main Street. It was another full blown intersection, with a complicated array of traffic signals. The red brick police/fire station and city hall was still on the corner. It was a square two-story tower with small flag on top. Was the library still on its second floor? Royce recalled the creaky wood floors and smell of mildew that permeated the library. It had a sad complement of aged books, most with frayed bindings, written by unknown authors and left leaning sideways on partly empty shelves. Didn't a cute girl work there? Across the street Elektra's restaurant was gone—burned to the ground, or so he'd heard soon after he left town. He and Toby worked there. Royce earned 40 cents an hour as a busboy and 60 cents an hour as a dishwasher. Good money for a 14-year-old at the time. "Worked my butt off, but I was able to buy a moped and set of drums," he recalled. It was now a gas station. A car horn jerked Royce back to reality and he waved, and turned left into town.

Algonquin was only two, maybe three blocks long and Royce was soon driving on the outskirts. After about a mile he spotted the dirty yellow bulb lit sign of the Algonquin Guest House, and pulled in.

The ignition off, Royce opened the door and stood stretching. It had become a cool summer evening, inky dark and quiet like the country. The Algonquin Guest House was a renovated multistory prairie Folk Victorian. It had a three-quarter veranda, with porch swing and wicker chairs, gables and some gingerbread in the eaves. The downstairs lights were on, but he couldn't see anyone moving about inside.

He shouldered his laptop and pulled his carry-on from the trunk and extended the handle. The first step let him know the bag wouldn't roll so smoothly across the gravel parking lot. He gave up and grabbed the handle. There was one other car in the lot, with license plates from Wisconsin.

Royce climbed the steps and across the veranda to the heavy oak door. It had a large oval window with frosted glass depicting a forest glen. He eased open the door to the living room.

Inside it was brightly lit and warm. The room was furnished in a hodge-podge of overstuffed chairs, a pair of couches and a coffee table piled with rumpled newspapers, magazines and a dried up bouquet of flowers. It smelled of fried food.

"Hello?" Royce called out. He heard water running in a back room.

No response. A room to the left had a computer on a small roll-top desk. The screen saver was bouncing a Chicago Cubs emblem across the black screen. From the living room a narrow flight of stairs, with a worn red oriental carpet, climbed to a second floor.

"Hello?" He called out a little louder. The water abruptly shut off.

From the dining area came a smallish middle-aged woman, wiping her hands on a dishrag.

"Hello, yes, I'm sorry," she said in a breathless and thin voice. "I was washing up in the kitchen and didn't hear you come in." She wiped her forehead with the back of her wrist.

"Not a problem," Royce said, smiling and bending a bit forward. "My name is Royce Partridge. I made a reservation over the internet."

"Oh yes." The woman stopped in front of him and extended a tiny hand. She couldn't have been five foot tall if she was on tiptoes. "You're the gentleman from New Jersey. My name is Dora Zetterberg. My husband Bill and I own the Algonquin Guest House." Then she quickly added. "Welcome. We were expecting you this afternoon?"

"Actually, I'm from Northern California."

He was met with a blank stare.

"I thought I put late arrival on the reservation."

Dora darted off to the office, saying over her shoulder. "Afternoon is a late arrival to us." She was back with a clipboard. "Please fill this out. And you reserved one or two nights?"

"Two nights," Royce said, taking the clipboard. He sat on a nearby chair and filled out the form.

Dora flitted from the office to the kitchen, to the living room while Royce scribbled name, address and so on. She had an instantly annoying habit of making sounds like a breathy whistle. If it was a tune it had no melody that Royce could recognize. He completed the form and pulled out his wallet for his credit card.

"I'm sorry. I don't know the license number of the car. It's a rental."

"Oh, that's alright," Dora said, taking the clipboard, credit card and zipping into the office.

Royce heard her at the computer keyboard, a dial tone, the swipe of the card and some beeps. Then she was back handing him his credit card and a large, heavy, old style brass key. He was putting his credit card back into his wallet and only vaguely heard her say that breakfast was from 7:30 to 9:30 every morning but Sunday.

"It's just Bill and me, and we serve cereal, toast, coffee, juice and eggs any way you like. Sort of continental, don'cha know."

Royce was turning the large heavy key over and over in his hand.

"We have you in the Salesman's Suite. It's at the top of the stairs and the first door to the left. You will know it by the valise on the door."

"No swipe cards?" He asked, hefting the key and giving her a smile.

"Oh, goodness no," She laughed. "We don't have anything like that here. The key is for the room only. The front door is usually unlocked until 11 at night. You can get in later by ringing the bell."

"Is it possible to get something to eat? I know it's late."

"Too late I'm afraid. I just finished the dishes and closed the kitchen for the night."

"Is there someplace near?" Royce asked, slinging his laptop, taking up his carry-on and going to the stairs.

"Well...there's the CarDunAl Lounge. It's open until midnight and has food. It's about half a mile east on 31."

"Thanks." Royce said climbing the stairs. "I will probably go out then."

"You are very welcome, Mr. Partridge. We will see you in the morning." And Dora disappeared around the corner into the kitchen.

The hall was dim, with a low watt bulb overhead. The door to the room had Salesman's Suite lettered in wood across the transom, with a wood cut-out of a red carpetbagger's valise. The large brass key rattled in the lock, and loosely clanked the bolt back. From a room down the hallway Royce heard a woman laugh.

It was a smallish L-shaped room, with more random furnishings and a large four poster bed. He looked, no TV. The bath had only a shower, toilet, sink and just enough room to turn right, then left, but not all the way round with your arms out. Royce put his laptop on a chair, heaved his carry-on onto the bed and unzipped it, taking his shaving kit to the bath. The window was shuttered and Royce opened the shutters and looked outside. There were shadowy images of the hills and scattered lights—but no vistas.

He checked his phone for messages and thought he should try to call Jessica again. He knew she would be irritated about his stopover in Algonquin and think the wrong thing. He didn't know why she should worry, though she was prone to it. Well, she'd have to worry another hour longer because he was hungry and wanted to get something to eat. He'd call her when he got back. Was there a phone in the room? No phone. He remembered the dial tone when Dora swiped his credit care. Dollars to doughnuts, he thought, there was no Wi-Fi. No TV, no phone, no Wi-Fi and no tub—they certainly took the comfort out of quaintness.

He slipped on a pair of jeans and t-shirt and locked the Salesman Suite behind him as he went down the stairs and to his car. The CarDunAl Lounge red neon sign was huge and it lit the parking lot in a pinkish hue.

The entrance to the CarDunAl Lounge (named for Carpentersville, Dundee and Algonquin) confused Royce for a moment. The entrance branched off in two directions; a lounge and a dining room. He opened the door and saw a bright room of tables with linen, service and candles, but absolutely no one dining. He looked around and didn't see any staff. Shrugging, he turned and went into the dimly lit lounge. Smoky and noisy, with a small combo on a corner stage, Royce could discern in the half-light a bar along one wall, stacks of bottles and backed by a mirror. The mirror reflected a orange gleam from the stage lights. Every once in awhile a shout or a laugh would cut through the darkness and rise above the din of the combo.

Getting accustomed to the dark Royce read a glossy placard with a photo near the end of the bar: Tonight Rosy Red and her Petals were featured. The picture on the placard and the faces of the band didn't exactly match, by about thirty years and a couple hundred gigs. The trio, shoulder to shoulder on a small corner stage had lost a lot in hair, but gained more in the belly. Did he used to play with any of these guys? Having been a drummer Royce checked out the drummer. He was overweight, bald and looked bored, with a cigarette hanging out his mouth. He had a mismatched kit: chrome snare, gold flake single tom

tom, blue pearl floor tom and stained wood kick drum, with high-hat, ride and small crash cymbals. It was a basic setup. And Rosy (who had appeared on television in episodes of Love, American-Style, Cannon and Hollywood a Go-Go according to the sign) still looked much the same if not rounder, with blonde bouffant hairdo and layers of pastel makeup. Even from across the lounge Royce could see the best of her was featured on the placard. She could really fill out the white fringe mini-dress and calf length white patent leather boots. Her tassels went wild as she growled out "*big wheel keep on turnin'...*"

There were shadowy figures slouched along the bar, and a few eyed Royce suspiciously as he blindly felt his way to a small round table. Elbows crooked, bottles in hand, they turned away.

A cocktail waitress came up. "What'll it be, hon?"

"Nothing for me," Royce said above the splash of a cymbal. "I'd like to get something to eat. Is the kitchen still open?" At that moment Rosy and her Petals stopped and Royce's voice was loud throughout the bar.

"Yeah, Hon," the waitress said. "Just go in the dining room and take a seat." She dismissed him with a flip of a cocktail napkin and a turn of her tray.

A little embarrassed, Royce made his way back out the bar and came blinking into the light of the dining room. He heard the combo trip over itself and tumble into another number. Rosy gave it her all. "*I was born in the wagon of a medicine show...*"

From the din, dim and sad air of the bar, the quiet and empty dining room was comforting. Royce went to the back and took a seat at a table by a window.

Finishing a conversation, a young girl with a blonde pony tail flying behind her, burst out of the kitchen and into the dining room. She crossed the room on quick feet.

"Sorry," she said breathlessly. "I didn't see you. We don't get too many people in here this late at night."

"No, it's fine," Royce replied, taking the laminated menu she offered.

"Sorry, but we closed down the grill...so all we can do ya are sandwiches or something."

Royce glanced up from the menu, not upset, just wondering why she handed him a menu if almost all of the dishes were off. She did sound truly sorry, and he noticed she blushed. A dipping glance and a flutter in her eyes confirmed it.

"Well, I would love a sandwich. What do you have?"

"Um...like roast beef or salami, maybe?" she said with a little laugh.

She couldn't have been more than seventeen, a fresh oval face with large blue eyes. There was a lot of Scandinavian blood in this area and he wondered if her surname ended with a gren, sen, son, man or berg. Slim, though still pudgy from baby fat, the bulky green sweater didn't give much away. She wiggled a bit under Royce's gaze, looked away, glancing up and down.

"Turkey?" he asked. "Can I get a turkey sandwich?"

She seemed relieved she had something to write on her pad. "Would you like soup also?"

"Sure," he said, handing the menu up. "What kind do you have?"

"There's clam chowder, minestrone and chicken noodle."

"Chowder?"

"No, it's real good. It's from a can."

"Chicken noodle will be fine. And can I get a beer?"

"You betcha. What kind do you want?'

"Well? What do you have?'

"Lots. Miller, Bud and Michelob."

There was a pause.

"That's lots?"

"Yeah."

"Michelob will be fine. With a glass." he said.

"I'll be right back with your beer," she said with a big smile. "And we'll have your sandwich and soup for you in a jiff."

Royce watched her go back to the kitchen. She had nice round hips, and a little jiggle. He turned to the window and blurry headlights crossed from one side to the other along Route 31. He realized, turning the gold band, he'd been flirting with her. I am old enough to be her father, no, wait, her grandfather, he thought with a twinge of shame.

"Here you go," she said heavy on the sweetness, placing a bottle of Michelob with an overturned glass on the neck before him.

"Thanks." Royce took the beer and tilting the glass, poured. She watched for a moment.

"You're not from around here, are you?"

"No…I'm not," he replied, filling the glass and giving her a little smile. "How did you know?"

"You don't look like nobody here—you're pretty skinny, and got a nice haircut. Most old guys around here look like they're three months pregnant." She giggled at her own joke. "You're polite. And they don't drink beer from a glass." She had a Midwestern naiveté, friendly and curious.

"I run. I'm seeing a friend in the hospital," he said in a flat tone that should've clued her he wanted to be alone. He looked back to the window, and she quietly slipped back into the kitchen.

The beer was cold and tasted good after his long day of travel.

In a few minutes she returned with a sandwich on a plate, steaming bowl of chicken noodle soup and potato chips in a bag.

"That looks delicious."

"What is your friend in the hospital for?" She asked, trying to rekindle the spark of their conversation. She waited for his response with her hands clasped and gently swaying her hips.

"Cancer," Royce responded in a monotone, chewing. It was the meant to be harsh.

"Oh, I'm sorry," she stammered, the enthusiasm drained from her voice. "Let me know if you need anything else." Embarrassed, she disappeared in a rush to the kitchen.

"Thanks. I will." And Royce was by himself again, and glad. He ate and thought about Toby, wondering what kind of cancer he was dying from. He'd find out tomorrow at the hospital.

He finished his meal, paid and left a good tip.

Back in the Salesman Suite, leafing through a McHenry County Chamber of Commerce brochure, Royce leaned back on the pillows of the four poster bed and called Jessica on his phone. She sounded sleepy.

"Hey...it's me. Fine. I know, I know, sorry. I thought you wanted me to call. No, I'm alright. It was a long flight, lots of turbulence and no food. Here? Seems about the same. It feels kind of weird, though. What? No...no old girlfriends. Come on, Jess—it's been forty years. They wouldn't remember me. Jess?" He took the cell away from his ear and glanced to the ceiling. "No...I came back to see Toby in the hospital...and Algonquin and the river again. I've told you about my friend Toby...and Frank, you know Frank, and a guy named Will. I haven't seen Toby in forty years. Frank said he was dying." She was talking, but he wasn't listening. "I'll be back Saturday night, yes, Saturday. You'll pick me up at the airport, right? I hate the shuttle. Okay, I'll take the shuttle. Yeah, okay...go back to sleep. Right, right, right...yeah, love you too. Bye." He pressed the button on his phone, tossed it onto the bed and fell back into the pillows with a sigh.

"Why the hell did I come back here?" he wondered aloud. In the quiet of the room he knew it was too late to question his snap decision to come back. He thought about seeing Toby again. What would it be like seeing him after all the years, and in the hospital dying of cancer.

He was sleepy and checked his watch. It was nearly midnight. He struggled up and took out his running gear from his carry-on and laid it out on a chair. He'd take a short run then go to the hospital. He went into the bathroom, brushed his teeth and took a piss. Yawning, scratching, he took off his clothes and tossed them over the back of the chair, then climbed into bed. He was tired. The turkey sandwich was sitting like a rock in his gut. He pulled the chain on the bedside lamp and lay in darkness, listening to the lullaby shush of highway traffic.

3

He dreamed a blur of faces and places, familiar, yet things he couldn't quite recall. When he woke, for a moment, he forgot he was in a B&B in Algonquin and might be late for work. Bright sunlight shone through the shuttered window with its beige flower print curtains. He could hear birds outside. His watch on the bedside table read 7:12 in the morning. It seemed earlier. Perhaps he was still on West Coast time.

Yawning, swinging his legs onto the floor, rubbing his face and sniffing, he looked around and saw himself in the dresser mirror and frowned. He swirled his tongue over sticky teeth and struggled up into a stretch. What a strange dream, he thought stumbling to the bathroom. Toby was driving and Royce was in the tiny back seat with a girl. They were double-dating on the way to the DunDale Drive-in. They laughed and laughed as Toby seemed to be shifting gears over and over with a long stick off the steering column. This wasn't three-on-the-tree, but endless shifting up and down. They were dressed in weird clothes, madras, minis, then in polka dots and paisley—pre-hippie garb. What the hell did that mean? He had no idea.

He thought of Toby in the hospital.

In the bathroom he doused his face with cold water, gave his hair a couple of swipes with his hands and brushed his teeth. He'd shower and shave after he got back from his run.

Wrestling on his T-shirt, supporter and running shorts, wrist band and half socks, he remembered the dream ended with the four of them staring at the big screen of the drive-in with James Bond in a tuxedo looking back at them, stirred but not shaken. He paused tying his running shoes. They were happy, he remembered as the sense he got waking from the dream.

"Jesus," he muttered, dropping the large brass key into an inside pocket of his shorts. "The coolest guy and the toughest guy I have ever known. But this cancer...."

A clear and cloudless blue sky--a summer morning with white dew on the grass and wetting the cars windshields, met him as he stepped off the veranda. The moist air touched him with a slight chill. It was typical for an August morning with Indian summer approaching. Royce took a few deep breaths, taking in the smell of gasoline and wet grass, then shook himself to loosen his muscles. He pushed against the trunk of his rental car—feeling a slight soreness as he stretched his hamstrings. He brought one foot forward, then the other, and held the position for a few seconds. He squatted until both knees almost touched the grease-stained gravel. He'd done this routine so many times he went through the stretches quickly and thoughtlessly. He hung over, stretching his lower back, touching his toes. After he straightened up, did a twist at the waist, took some quick short breathes and told himself: "Go."

No matter the years and years he'd been running, starting out was always the hardest. Just getting out of the B&B parking lot and dodging early morning bumper-to-bumper traffic crossing Route 31 was a difficult task. "Stop," was something he would tell himself over and over. But he went on knowing from all the times in the past, if he gave in and quit, he would feel guilty. It was just something he had to run through. The low sun, warm on his face, the dew cold and wet on his ankles, pleased him. He trotted along the gravel shoulder of the road, with the flow of traffic. Cars whizzed by at high speed, carelessly close. His knees were aching a bit; he was getting winded, and sweat was running down his neck and back. He knew that would go away soon. But he had to keep at it.

He turned onto Main Street, and the houses started to get older, more distinct. These were historic houses, prairie Victorians from the late 19th century. White washed, two-story, L-shaped and austere with two story carriage houses in the back. The houses lacked the flair of San Francisco Victorians of the era; yet, they had a certain character, the hardy, no nonsense Midwestern quality of the pioneers and middleclass merchants.

A block down he could see the pointed spire of a church. He thought it may have been the Lutheran church he remembered from so many years ago. He made a mental note to stop in. It was, if still the same after all this time, a very spare and simple church, with only a cross backlit on a white background and no suffering Jesus hung there to remind him of his own pain. A Lutheran Christ appeared more put-out about the whole nailed to the cross thing.

His breathing relaxed, the sweat cooled and his knees and joints no longer ached. Royce was past the discomfort, pressing himself to recall a history lesson from Junior High. Indians lived here and along the banks of the Fox River until they were chased out following defeat in the Blackhawk War. The name of the tribe he struggled to remember—Potto-something, Potawatomi Indians. The first white man in the area built a log cabin on the northern edge of town, on the crest of the valley where Route 31 and Cary Road met, and where Algonquin's oldest cemetery is laid out. This was also the site of an Indian burial ground known as the Algonquin Mounds. Originally, the town was called Cornish Ferry, after a doctor who settled in the area in the early 1800s. The only reason Royce recalled this was because Doc Cornish was the town's first postmaster, then sheriff and later coroner. On a history test Royce had written he 'birth'em, mailed'em, jailed'em and when all was said and done--nailed'em. The teacher wrote *how droll* but Royce got a B.

After Cornish Ferry the town's name changed to Osceola, for no apparent reason. When the town fathers learned another town in Illinois had a prior claim to the name it was suggested the town be named Algonquin after the confederation of Indian tribes that had lived in the Midwest. That had always struck Royce as ironic, steal the

Indians' land, but name towns after them. Algonquin means "across the water" which is where the Indians would have preferred the Europeans had remained.

A teenager riding a decal decorated, fluorescent red and green spray painted skateboard cut sharp switchbacks left, then right, then around Royce and down the Main Street sidewalk, ignoring the NO SKATEBOARDING stenciled on the pavement. He was nearing the business district, all three or four blocks of it. The yellow brick Algonquin National Bank—"now with 8 locations to serve you" was on the same corner, across from the corner drugstore. The corner drugstore had cast iron steps and a rounded turret on its second floor. Royce wondered about the five dollars he left in his bank account some forty years ago. "Let's see," he mused. "At 5.5 percent, compounded annually, for forty years, that would be...that would be....aw, to heck with it."

The sidewalks downtown were about two feet above street level. That was from long ago, when sidewalks needed to be high to load the horse-drawn farm wagons. He could see it, and loved the confusion of now and the past in the town architecture. Across the street the brown wood post office, with its smallish framed windows, looked as if it had been left over from the late 19th century. This was where he got his social security card at fourteen; and his draft card at eighteen. If he had time, he would go and see if the counter still had frosted glass and narrow windows with tarnished brass bank bars.

He jogged by three farmers going into a coffee shop. Two were about Royce's age, hefty and dressed in faded overalls; one wore a beat-up green and gold John Deere cap, the other in a blue Cubs baseball cap. The third was younger, the next generation in jeans and a Pink Floyd Dark Side of the Moon T-shirt, his long hair tied in a pony tail. All three gave Royce a sidelong glance as they went past. He wondered if many people ran around there, or if the San Francisco Half-Marathon T-shirt threw them.

Surprisingly, quite a few of the stores and shops Royce recognized from so many years ago. Buffalo's Main Street Market still boasted "Half Cattle & Hindquarters custom cut for home freezer." The Algonquin Bakery seemed familiar, though he wasn't sure and it may have been the smell of freshly baked bread. The Growl'n Snarl pet shop and Prince Fong's Chinese take-away were most definitely new to Royce. But Haag Hardware had been on Main Street for decades, long before Royce had ever set foot in Algonquin. In fact, the Haags were prominent and prolific, with namesakes all over the valley. There were Haags in his junior high and high school classes. But what happened to the Ben Franklin's Five and Dime or Eddy's Soda Shoppe? Eddy's Arm Pit as it was affectionately known, he wondered had he missed it? Or was it also gone?

Green canvas pennants faded whitish by the sun, hung limp on the lampposts proclaiming Algonquin's Founder's Days. Founder's Days was held annually at the end of July. Royce thought about Toby, the year his softball team won town championship for 16-inch softball. Royce stood at second base, while Toby got all the praise. Frank won the 6K fun run that year; while Will was the pie-eating champ. Royce got a second place ribbon for a poem about

Algonquin. It was only second place but he got some merciless first place caliber teasing from his pals, not so much for writing a poem, more so for finishing in second place.

The Founder's Day parade was a succession of the junior and senior high school bands, separated by horses and riders in old west rhinestone regalia, tractors with hay floats depicting smiling and waving settlers and Indians, the Odd Fellows, VFW, Kiwanis, Lions, Rotary, American Legion and Jaycees in dealership convertibles, then the mayor and other town officials, with the town's fire trucks closing the show.

Royce turned onto Chicago Street, the end of Route 62, which he'd come in on last night.

There was always a street dance the last night of Founder's Days. Royce smiled, vividly recalling the used car lot on the corner cleared of cars and decorated with Christmas lights. An amped up sound system blasted Eddie Cochran's *Summertime Blues*. Older couples danced. Little kids ran through the dancers. Groups of teenage girls clustered on one side. While the boys eyed them, longing, trying to pluck up the courage to cross what seemed terrifying miles to ask for a dance.

The sun was higher, the day heating up as the morning dew burned off.

He was on his second wind, his breath regular and running with an effortless stride. His mind wandered.

The concrete bridge that spanned the Fox River was built in the early 1930s, probably as a WPA project during the depression. It was either poorly planned by the builders, or decades of a subtle shifting of the river bank had caused the bridge to jut nearly half a foot above the roadbed. The four-lane road had been patched again in an effort to have the road and bridge meet. There was still a sharp bump up and clunk down when a car drove over the bridge. Royce leapt onto the bridge walkway and looked down at the river.

The river roared over a spillway that maintained the Fox at a depth of about five feet north from Algonquin to the first set of locks up river in McHenry. The brown water moved placidly to the dam and then turned nasty, churning white water and roaring over the dam. There were always objects caught in the foamy backwash, usually logs, boat cushions, chunks of Styrofoam, rolling over and over until they broke apart or became waterlogged and sunk. Below the dam the Fox became as shallow as a creek, meandering its rocky way south through cornfields and cow pasture down to Elgin.

The reverberating cry of a crow from beneath the bridge startled Royce. He slowed and watched as the huge black bird glided down river, beneath a leafy canopy of trees and spraying water rainbows. The glinting sunlight making its jet black feathers shine like silver. The bird lazily flapped its wings, dipped and lighted onto a long branch downstream.

Royce paused, remembering.

Rolling in the back flow of the dam was a big log. At least that's what Royce thought it was when first he saw it. He eased his bicycle to a stop and leaned it against the buttress. Whatever it was it was white and spotted brown, fat and round as it turned slowly over and over and under the cascading water. A group of boys about Royce's age were on the far bank shouting, laughing, throwing rocks at the log. Most of the rocks sailed high and wide of the log, except for those hurled by a blond boy. He had a smooth throwing motion and repeatedly hit the turning log. Each time the log made a deep, resounding thump, like a tympani drum. It would echo off the bridge and among the rush of the water.

It wasn't until four stiff and skinny legs rolled up and out of the backflow that Royce realized it wasn't a log at all, but some sort of animal. The animal's head came round and he saw it was a cow, bloated to twice its normal size. The cow's brown eyes bugged out with a dumb glassy look and its tongue was stuck out swollen and black. He'd never seen anything like it and was more curious than repelled by the sight.

A blond boy scrambled up the bank with an armful of rocks and was approaching where Royce stood. He was about Royce's height, dressed in a striped T-shirt and cut-off jeans. He wore a pair of dirty low-top Converse sneakers with no socks. What struck Royce immediately was his dark tan and quick, friendly smile.

"Pretty cool, huh?" he said excitedly, nearing Royce. "It must've drowned up the river and floated down stream." He dropped his load of rocks and hefted one to throw.

Royce was self-conscious, shy, and struggled for something to say other than—"Yeah, pretty cool."

The boy let fly a rock that cracked off the passing hoof of the cow. Other boys on the bank cheered.

Royce wanted to be friendly, but was tongue-tied.

"I've seen you before. You just moved to Algonquin, didn't you?" the boy said. "Off River Road."

"Yeah," he replied, wondering how the boy knew.

"I live off River Road too," the boy said, throwing a rock that thumped off the cow's round belly. "I saw you move in. My name's Toby Bergman."

He felt more relaxed and was relieved Toby was leading the conversation. "Hey. My name's Royce Partridge. We moved in a couple of weeks ago."

"Royce? That's an odd name. How'd you get that?" Toby's broad smile disarmed any offense Royce might've taken.

"It was my mom's last name--some kind of family tradition."

"Well, it's not as bad as Tobias," he said, throwing a rock hard, missing the cow completely. "Tobias Bergman-- the third!"

"Toby's a cool name," Royce said quietly, looking down at the cow rolling over and over.

"Thanks," Toby said, brushing back a shock of blond hair. "That's Frank over there, the skinny guy," pointing out a boy on the bank. "And the big clod is Will...but don't ever call him Willy," he added, pointing to a second boy. Those other guys are from Lake in the Hills.

Lake in the Hills was the next town north.

"You going to Algonquin High?"

"Yeah...ninth grade," Royce replied, feeling more at ease. "What about you?"

"Yup." Toby was nearly out of rocks. He threw three in rapid succession. All three thumped and bounced wildly off the swollen cow. "It's full of gas and I want to blow it up," he said. "C'mon down and meet the guys."

"I can't," Royce lied, turning his bike, anxious at the thought of meeting strangers. "I've got to go to the store for my mom."

"Okay. Hey," Toby said, running down the bridge. "We'll come over sometime."

Royce froze inside, afraid. Toby was already at the other end of the bridge and it was too late to tell him not to come to his house. He liked Toby at once. He would've liked to have Toby as a friend. But he knew he couldn't have friends.

There was always the fear, Royce recalled as he started jogging again. He slowed and waited for a break in traffic. The fear someone would find out about his parents drinking. It was easier not to have friends. He dashed through a gap in the traffic and onto River Road.

It was much the same as Royce remembered. Tall trees lined the shoulder and along the river bank, with long leafy limbs over the narrow asphalt. It was late summer and the leaves had started losing the deep green of spring and summer. Soon the leaves would be turning from faint green to burnt orange, amber, red and yellow. Most of the homes along the road were older, up the valley wall and surrounded by bushes, hedges and trees. The newer homes, usually single level ranch-style, were fronted by manicured lawns.

Nearly every property had a cleared area on the river bank, with a dock or 'beach'. The beaches were usually small pebbles or river rock. The size and type of boat tied up to the piers, from runabouts to cabin cruisers, was a pretty good indication of the wealth of the property owner. And there were some huge boats rocking at berth. Often, a green scum line on the white fiberglass hulls told of the owners neglect.

Royce ran along the shady road. It was cool in the shade of the trees. A small speed boat was tearing up river with its outboard loudly humming. There was a familiar house, the Welanders. Well, it was the Welanders house when he was seventeen years old. Hot summer nights he'd slip up to Judy Welander's bedroom window and lightly tap on the glass, careful not to wake her parents in the corner bedroom. She'd pretend to be sleeping, though he knew she lay awake waiting for him. Sometimes she'd come out and they would go down to the river and talk for hours. And other times, she'd open the window then stand back as Royce quietly climbed in. In the half-light she'd stand naked before him. They would lie side by side on her single bed. There were women's cosmetics on the bedside dresser, and little girls' stuffed animals in the corner of her bed.

"She was beautiful," he remembered, "I never forgot her."

Wood Street branched off River Road and curved up the valley. On this street Royce's parents had built a house for about $30,000, an exorbitant sum in the mid-sixties. A raised ranch, three bedroom, three-bath home on a quarter acre of rough land. The house had some classy features, a slate foyer which his mother insisted on, full basement, flagstone fireplace and all sorts of modern kitchen gadgetry. The single-most eye-catching feature of the house was its beamed cathedral ceiling in the living room and a wall of windows overlooking the river.

Royce hesitated at the bottom of Wood Street, uncertain if he wanted to see the house after all the years. He had no idea how many hands it'd gone through since his parents divorce. His father had sold it in the mid 1970s. There was no doubt, nothing even remotely related to him and all the years his family had lived there. It was other peoples' home, not his.

But, he'd come all this way, even if he was going to have to run uphill, he had to see the house. Royce set off and found the road a steeper climb than he recalled. He was getting breathless. Wood Street was still being developed when the Partridge family moved in. The sites were all blocked out, but it had only about four houses when Royce left.

"Oh my god," he whispered in shock. "It's painted black."

He stopped, hands on knees, catching his breath. He wanted to be inconspicuous, but the change from a light green wood stain to shiny black, startled him. It was still the same house. Surveying the tall trees in the yard Royce realized he'd planted the 30-plus foot fir tree in the side yard when he was 14 years old. And the thick trunked birch tree was but a spindly yard high sapling when he'd dug the hole in the center of the front lawn for its burlap bound root ball. He felt very old and sad. There were plots of grass on the sloping hillside that he'd sweated over seeding and wrestling a roller on. If he mowed on Saturday he got a couple of bucks and maybe the use of the car for a date—if his father didn't get too drunk and renege on it all.

A BMX bike was carelessly laid on the lawn.

For a brief moment it occurred to him to knock on the door and ask the current owners if he could look inside. But the thought of walking around the house and all the memories it would bring back, of yelling and punches and slaps of drunken fights between his mother and father, dissuaded him. He would recall every broken window, door a fist had gone through, cigarette burns on the carpet and blood on the white tile kitchen, in the house where the curtains were drawn and visitors not welcome.

He'd seen enough, turned and jogged down the hill.

A sharp knock on the front door made Royce jump. He dashed from the television to the door where he recognized Toby. He saw Royce, so he couldn't pretend no one was home. He hesitantly opened the door.

"Hey," he cautiously said.

"Hey," Toby said happily. Will and Frank waved from down the driveway, standing by a pair of mopeds.

Royce slipped out the door, closing it behind him. "What're you guys doing?" He tried to sound nonchalant, but inside he was scared their knocking had awakened his mother from her drunken stupor. What if she started yelling? Worse yet, with Toby and the others on the front step, she might come staggering out of the bedroom half-dressed, bedraggled and reeking of booze.

Toby motioned toward a tall, beefy boy with greased back black hair and pimply complexion. "This is Will...and Frank." He was shorter than the other two, skinny, with a prominent nose and lips.

"Hey. I'm Royce."

"Yeah, we know," Will said gruffly, sauntering down the driveway. "Wow, this is some house. Can we see inside?"

"No...not now," Royce said quickly, taking a step back, blocking the way to the door. "You can't come in." Toby and the others gave him a quizzical look. "My mom's sick, got the flu."

"So?" Will took a step toward the door.

Royce faced him, panicked inside. He couldn't risk it. "She's sleeping." A long moment passed, with Will staring at Royce like he was strange.

"We're going down to Eddy's," Toby broke in. "C'mon, Royce."

Still in fear but dazed by the sudden turn, he let Toby pull him away from the door. The others ran for their moped.

If Toby had known, he never let on.

"Last guy pays!" Frank shouted, hopping onto Will's Moped. And the race was on. They pedaled their Sears Allstate 50cc mopeds and started up the 2-stroke engines. Toby motioned to Royce. "Hop on the back." And in a cloud of oily blue smoke Toby revved up the engine with its high-pitched whine then tore down the driveway and onto

Wood Street. "Hold onto the back of the rack," he said over the engine noise.

They met up at the bottom of Wood Street at River Road. Will was looking back and once Toby and Royce reached them, he took off toward town. Jockeying back and forth, they raced as much as they could given the 35 mph top speed of the mopeds. Stopping at the intersection of River Road and the highway, they waited for a break in the stream of cars coming down the hill. They revved the high-pitched engines until they were nearly engulfed by blue exhaust.

"How come it's so smoky?" Royce yelled in Toby's ear.

"We use boat gas, instead of mixing it," Toby said. "Hold on," he added as they zoomed onto the highway and the Fox River bridge.

Royce saw Will bump off the other side of the bridge, and Frank almost bounce off the back. He didn't need Toby's warning to "get ready" when they hit the bump.

They raced through town and pulled up in front of Eddy's Soda Shoppe and News Agency. The store front had a shiny green plastic screen pulled down to block out the afternoon sun.

Will was laughing. "I almost lost you," he said to Frank.

"You did that on purpose," Frank said as they went into Eddy's.

Eddy's was narrow, with one side all newspaper and magazine racks; the other side was a long pale blue counter and soda fountain. A couple sat at the end of the counter eating hamburgers and French fries. They must've asked for well done burgers because there was a faint stink of burnt meat. Two ceiling fans in the front and back slowly turned. A man in blue jeans and flannel shirt was down toward the back of the magazine racks, leafing through a men's magazine. A long coil of sticky brown flypaper hung in the corner. It was the last stop for quite a few flies, although more had survived to fly loops around the shop.

Toby, Royce, Will and Frank sat at the counter on low, round swivel seats. Will spun in his seat. There was a miniature jukebox on the counter and Royce flipped through the selections.

"What can I do you for boys?" a tall, skinny, grey haired man in a brown splotched apron asked.

"I'll have a cherry phosphate," Toby said.

"Me too," Will chimed in, spinning by.

"I'd like a green river," Frank said.

"Just a Coke for me," Royce added. "In the bottle."

"Coming right up, boys."

"Thanks Eddy," Toby said.

"I'm not Eddy," the man wearily said, walking away.

Frank whispered something to Will which made him exclaim. "Not again? This is the tenth time you've come here and not have any money. I'm not going to pay for your drink."

"I'll pay for his," Royce volunteered.

"There you go," Will said to Frank. "You lucked out again."

"So...Royce," Toby asked. "Where did you move from?"

"It was a town south of Chicago, around Chicago Heights," he replied.

"Nice place?" Will asked.

"I guess," Royce said. "It was kind of a boring, fake, manufactured suburb. I didn't like it much and was glad when we moved."

The man who wasn't Eddy set three paper cones of drinks and a bottle of Coke before the boys.

"How come?" Toby wondered, sucking at the straw in his drink.

"It was," Royce took a sip of his Coke, swallowed and said, "a really snotty, middle-class place. There were cliques at school and if you were different you were looked down on."

"You miss your buddies from back there?" Frank asked.

"I didn't really have any buddies."

"What? No friends?" Toby was astonished. "Man, I've known these two farmers since grade school."

"Well, I was the kid their parents told them they couldn't play with."

Frank leaned forward and looked up the counter at Royce. "Who? You?"

"Yeah, they thought I was a troublemaker," Royce said and looked down at his Coke. "There was some stuff that happened. I didn't do it, but I got blamed for it."

"Wha'cha do, kill somebody?" Will laughed.

"Naw, it was nothing."

"You're not going to tell us," Toby said, with a half smile. "Are you?"

"Nope, I'm not."

"We'll get it out of you," Will said teasing.

"Sooner or later..." Frank started to say.

"Anyway," Royce interrupted. "My dad got transferred to Des Plaines and I was glad to move."

"To Algonquin?" Will exclaimed. "There's nothing going on around here."

"I like that," Royce said. "This is a cool town. It's old. And there's the river."

"Is that your dad's boat at the dock on River Road?" Toby asked.

"Yeah," Royce replied. "Sixteen-foot Thompson runabout with a 60-horse Evinrude."

"That ought to pull a skier," Toby said to Will and Frank, then turned to Royce. "Does your dad let you take it out on the river?"

"Sometimes," Royce lied, knowing his father had never let him take his boat out without him. "I know where the key is, though."

"Let's go water skiing tomorrow," Toby suggested.

"I'm for that," Frank interjected.

"I'm not very good at it," Royce said.

"Don't worry," Will put in, "Toby is a great water skier. He'll teach you."

"I can't ever use my dad's boat," Toby said shaking his head.

"It's a big one," Frank added.

"A twenty-one foot cabin cruiser, sleeps four, with a hundred horse Mercury."

"You guys got boats?" Royce asked Will and Frank.

"Naw," Frank spoke up. "Will and I live across the highway, in the subdivision by the high school."

Royce took a quarter from his pocket and dropped it into a slot at the top of the miniature jukebox on the counter. "Anybody want to hear something?" Royce asked. "It's three plays for a quarter."

"Beach Boys," Toby said quickly.

Royce punched in *Surfin' Safari*. He glanced over to Will and Frank, and they both shrugged. "Nothing?" Royce leafed through the slates, then selected Chuck Berry's *Roll Over Beethoven* and *I Want to Hold Your Hand* by The Beatles.

Softly, in the background, a guitar riff started.

"Beach Boys," Toby happily said.

"Naw, it's Chuck Berry," Royce corrected.

"Sounds like the Beach Boys..."

"Ya think?" Royce replied.

Then Chuck Berry started singing *Gonna write a little letter, mail it to my local DJ* and Toby said "Oh yeah...that's not the Beach Boys."

Royce and Toby became friends quickly. And though Toby was outgoing with a smile that could light up a room and Royce was brooding and reserved, they were very alike in a lot of ways. Will was the big, genial kid, with a ready laugh, but mean streak simmering just below the surface. If you were in a fix and needed a friend, Will would be there for you. He had a bad complexion over chubby cheeks, and was very self-conscious about it. Frank was the conservative one, cautious and less adventurous. The others constantly made fun of him because of this. And if Frank's didn't like something you might never hear the end of it.

The sum of the parts, Toby and Royce, Will and Frank, created the whole of the gang.

They spent the remainder of the afternoon at Eddy's, drinking sodas, talking, laughing and getting to know each other. Then later, they got back on the mopeds and Toby, Will and Frank took Royce on a tour of Algonquin.

By the dockside at the bottom of Wood Street, Royce stopped and stood on the bank. The late morning sun cast glittering light across the brown river. It was wide at this point, about half a mile to the other bank. He looked around and didn't see anyone. He stepped and slipped down the steep gravel bank and walked out to the end of the pier.

In the 17th century the French trapped fur and explored this region searching for the source of the Mississippi River and Indians to catholicize. They called it Riviere des Renard, after the Fox Indians who were massacred in the area.

The Fox was a tamed river, rarely overflowing its banks, nor varying in depth from a few feet to about 12 feet, regardless of spring thaw or fall rains. A series of locks and dams from the Chain O' Lakes down through Algonquin ensured the Fox never amounted to more than a lazy muddy river until it emptied into the Illinois River at Ottawa. The river was never exploited like other rivers. It didn't cross any coal fields and there were few factories along its Illinois run. Tug boats pushed long lines of coal barges up and down the Rock, the Des Plaines and the Illinois rivers, but there was never any commerce on the Fox. Those rivers went through the farm and industrial centers of Rockford, Peoria, Joliet and Chicago and merged into the mighty Mississippi River. But the Fox was too far north of Chicago and too shallow. If anything it was used as a sewer and spillage for tanneries and pulp mills up north in Wisconsin. And so it remained for generations, slow, neglected, and used primarily for recreation.

Little had changed since Royce had spent idyllic summer days on the river with Toby, Will and Frank. Nearly every day they would be on the river, swimming, water skiing or just hanging out. Summer cottages and houses dotted the opposite shoreline. Down by the bridge, in town, was River Vista, a ramshackle green clapboard tavern, with boat launch and dock. Across the river was a marina, as before. Only now it was Bergman's Marina. Bergman's Marina? Did he dare go see if it was owned by Toby?

Royce sat down at the end of the dock. A line of cars moved up the opposite side of the valley, climbing out of Algonquin on highway 31 toward Cary, McHenry and Crystal Lake. The river moved slowly along, below his dangling feet. It was green all up and down the banks from bushes, trees and lawns. Bright colors from the houses and docks dappled the greenery.

It was peaceful now, but come Saturday or Sunday this stretch of river from Algonquin north became as crowded and chaotic as a New Delhi roundabout. Boats of all shapes, sizes and horsepower, seaworthy or not; rafts and inner tubes; kayaks and canoes; hydroplanes with water skiers and brave little sailboats, all ran up and down the river like there was only 4 hours to a day. Royce and his friends rarely took to the river on weekends. "Too many amateurs," Toby said shaking his head in disgust. It was true. There were weekend boat collisions, horrific injuries to water skiers, boats sinking and capsizing with the occasional drowning. And at least once a season someone got too close to the spillway under the bridge and was pulled over. The combination of boat gas, alcohol and an open throttle marred for many what should have been a leisurely and fun weekend on the river. Royce's father was one of the culprits. He couldn't drive a car when drunk, though he often did, defying common sense and the law; but he sure could take their runabout out on the river, open the throttle and swerve in and out of other boats like a maniac.

Royce squinted up at the blue of the sky, then down to the green of the valley with it all underlined by the slow roll of this tranquil brown river. Ironic, but Algonquin was the kind of American small town that most kids couldn't wait to leave. They would reach age and were gone to college, military or following their wanderlust. (Royce had to admit, he had been one.) But as the hectic rush of years streamed past in a blur, the tranquil small town life, this lazy river, became moments he savored in quiet remembrance. He never appreciated it until it was gone. It was a simpler time, when life was out there for the taking and being young, he wasn't coerced by the complications and responsibilities of adulthood. Royce looked up river. His fondest memories seemed to flow from this river.

4

"We rode those damn mopeds everywhere. We weren't old enough to drive..." he remembered, smiling.

The sun was hot on Royce's sweaty face as he leaned against a piling. The river was cool and quietly lapped against the hull of a swaying boat. The ropes of its moorings creaked, and the tires lashed to the dockside squealed against the gunwales. Tar, boat gas and the reek of river mud was in his nostrils. Water plashed in the middle of the river as a fish jumped. Tangles of common brown grackles chattered and swooped from tree to tree along the banks. A blue-winged green-headed dragonfly hovered just above the water. All Royce's worries seemed insignificant at this moment. If it could always be this, he'd never leave. Memories ran like children charging downstairs on a Christmas morning. This river—always this lazy brown river--flowed through his thoughts. It reminded him of excitement and promise when his life was spread before him like a book of blank pages just waiting to be filled. Now it seemed he wore a heavy cloak of pessimism rather than the careless clothes of summery optimism from long ago.

Somewhere up river a boat chugged along. He imagined a rusted-out gut bucket of a barely seaworthy boat, with an ancient cough and wheeze outboard, so leaky it was barely able to keep afloat, but afloat nonetheless.

A group of boys on BMX bikes raced past on River Road. Royce opened his eyes and without turning his head imagined the boys churning by. It reminded him of the mornings Toby, Will and Frank would meet him at the dock. They'd take out Royce's father's runabout, water skiing until their arms ached from holding the tow rope. Usually, they'd run out of gas and have to catch a tow back to Algonquin. Sometimes it was the McHenry County Sheriff's patrol boat that would tow them. The old sheriff, with probably the best duty in the county, would admonish them, "I can't keep doing this for you boys." But he always did.

Royce could never get the hang of one ski. Toby, it went without saying, was a master at it.

It was a summer night and Royce slipped out the basement door into the darkness, knowing he didn't need to be so cautious, as all the lights upstairs were on and his parents were shouting from one end of the house to the other. "What was it tonight?" he wondered, emerging from the shadows along the house and onto Wood Street. Car? Bills? Kitchen? Kid? Did he threaten to hit her again, or was that another door being slammed? Sex? How they loathed each other. Yet they seemed to thrive on it. He needed to get out and they wouldn't notice him gone tonight, maybe not tomorrow either. He was the link in the chain that kept them shackled. He knew this from his father's cold hateful stare; and felt it in his mother's guilty tears.

"Fuck it," he spat into the shadows, walking down Wood Street.

This was Toby's crazy idea and he'd been talking to Royce about it for weeks. He liked the idea, desperate for some wild adventure to break the monotony of his sad life. Besides, they'd be back in school in a couple of weeks and no summer was complete without something to defy their parents and maybe even bend the law. Toby had only told Will and Frank part of the plan, knowing Will would object and Frank would find some excuse to not be there.

The night was breezy and warm, with a three-quarter moon hanging above the valley wall, drifting through scattered white puffs. His parents screaming grew faint behind him, and Royce became less tense. He wore cut-offs white jeans, holey low-top sneakers and a blue and red striped, oversized surfer style T-shirt. He'd brought along a zipper front, hooded grey sweatshirt, tied around his waist, even though the night was comfortable.

He reached the bottom of Wood Street and saw no one waiting under the yellow circle of streetlight on River Road. Maybe he was early? He was disappointed. Had they left without him? He thought he'd wait awhile longer then, and if he had to, go back home and watch TV. Maybe tonight he could get some sleep.

"Royce!" someone hissed from bushes behind him.

He started and wheeled about.

Out of the bushes they scrambled, laughing.

"Ha, scared the shit out of you!" Will said.

"Did not."

"Quiet," Frank cautioned.

Toby came up close to Royce. In the streetlight Royce noticed he was giving him arched eyebrows and a conspiratorial smirk. "We could hear your parents all the way down here. Do they always fight like that?"

Royce shrugged.

"You ready for this?" Toby asked.

With a crooked smile and slow nod Royce replied, "Oh yeah. You bet."

They set off down River Road, so excited they broke into a trot. Frank would accelerate the pace until they got winded and yelled at him to slow down. Frank ran track and never got winded. Whenever he started running ahead Will would get pissed off and make Toby and Royce stop with him. Frank, glancing back, seeing they weren't even trying to keep up, would stop.

"Did you tell Will and Frank the plan?" Royce breathlessly asked Toby as they jogged along.

"Well," he said, pausing. "Not all of it. Only that we were going to Recharge Resort, steal some canoes and go out on the river."

Every so often they'd spot car headlights coming towards them on the road.

"Car!"

They'd dive off the road for cover, waiting for the car to pass.

Recharge Resort was a mile or so down River Road, but they reached it in what seemed minutes. It was a charity resort for inner city kids from the Chicago area, and it had just closed for the season. They crouched low in the shadows by the nine-foot chain link fence, peering into the pitch dark. Only the caretaker's house, high up the hillside, was lit. All the tiny cabins neatly lined up the slope were dark.

"Shit," Frank whispered. "The old caretaker is home."

"He's deaf as a post."

"Yeah, but his German shepherd isn't."

"I don't see any canoes," Royce said.

"You need glasses?" Toby whispered. "There. See the silvery things on the rack by the swimming pool?"

"Oh...yeah."

"Maybe this isn't such a hot idea," Will's voice cracked. "How're we going to get the canoes out of there?"

"Cool it," Toby said in an impatient tone. "Royce and I will climb the fence. You two stay out here." They listened intently, moonlight shining in the whites of their big eyes. "We tip the canoe over the fence. You catch it and take it to the river bank. Then come back for the second one." Toby explained his plan as if it were a simple task, easily accomplished. Yet, as he spoke, his voice wavered.

"Okay," Frank said, struggling to sound composed. "What if we get caught?"

Will punched his shoulder. "You're such a 'mo. We aren't getting caught."

Toby and Royce grappled over the swaying chain link fence. They leapt to the soft dirt inside the resort. Royce looked back and saw the shadows of Will and Frank kneeling. It felt cold, dark and odd inside the resort. His stomach was trembling, his heart pounding. Part of him knew this was idiotic, trouble and wanted to get out of there. But the other half was willing to dare anything rather than let Toby down. They crept across the grounds to the canoe rack, keeping their eyes on the caretaker's house. Lace curtains billowed out an open window. A flickering blue-grey square of light from a TV could be seen reflected in the window glass. The sound was way up and they could hear the theme music for Mister Ed.

"We're in luck," Toby whispered. "They're not locked."

"...Willllllbbbbuuuuurrrrr," Royce whispered.

Toby stifled a laugh, sputtering out "shut-up".

These were nearly brand new shiny aluminum two-man canoes, resting upside down on a double rack. Orange life jackets and wooden paddles were stacked alongside.

"Didn't think of that. What if they were locked?"

"We'd be shit out of luck, and on our way home," Toby grinned. "Let's get the bottom two."

With Royce at the bow and Toby at the stern they slowly raised the canoe off the rack and eased it back and then over their heads, walking down to Frank and Will.

"Hurry up," They could hear Frank whispering.

"Don't trip." Toby said.

"It's lighter than I thought it'd be."

"Car!"

Toby and Royce froze with the canoe over their heads. Frank and Will disappeared into bushes.

The car went by fast—a flash of white light in the trees, a radio blasting *Little Deuce Coupe*—and the red glow from its tail lights.

"I know that guy."

Will was standing on the other side, hands on hips, looking skeptical, when Royce and Toby reached the fence.

"No way," he was shaking his head. "No way, we can't get that over the fence.

"No sweat," Royce said. "We'll tip it up and over the fence."

"Walk backwards to the end," Toby added.

Royce walked his hands down the canoe gunwales while Toby held the end. With the front angled up they rested the middle on the top of the fence. The light canoe was awkward and heavy in this position. Toby was puffing, struggling to hold the end down.

"Will," Royce said. "You've got to catch the end of the when we tip it over. Frank, you walk to the front. You've got to keep it off the fence or it'll make noise."

"Gotcha."

"Let's hurry," Frank said anxiously. "I think I hear a car."

"There's no car," Will said to Frank.

Royce helped Toby push the canoe end up. It left their fingertips and balanced on the fence. For a split second the canoe teetered between Royce and Toby and Will and Frank's outstretched arms. Then the front went down into

Will's grasp with a thud. Frank was under the canoe quickly, and silently eased it off the fence.

"Awright!" Royce softly said.

He and Toby dashed back to the canoe rack as Will and Frank, with the canoe over their heads, scuttled across River Road and down the embankment.

"Piece of cake," Toby said gleefully. It was easier now. He and Royce deftly hefted the second canoe and were at the fence in moments. Once they tipped it up and rested the middle on the fence, Royce hustled back for paddles and a couple of life jackets.

Toby pushed the back end up. Will waited on the other side as the front dipped down. Just as he got hold of the front Frank called out "is that a car?" Will turned his head, lost his grip and the canoe slid over the fence.

SCREEEEEEECH!

It seemed to loudly echo across the valley.

The caretaker's dog was at the open window barking.

"Shit shit shit," Toby was saying as he vaulted the fence and helped Will get the canoe off the road.

Bright light seemed to explode all over the resort. A dead bolt clattered. At least Royce thought the sound of chuk-chuk was a dead bolt being pulled back.

"Frank," Royce called, running to the fence. "Catch." And he tossed the paddles and life jackets over. Then hit the dirt. So did Frank.

"WHO'S OUT THERE?," the caretaker shouted, standing in the open back door—a tall, black silhouette with a leaping, barking dog at his hand and the unmistakable shape of a shot gun in the other.

Will and Toby had managed to get the canoe across the road and down to the river bank just before the caretaker came out. Frank and Royce lay alongside each other, separated by the fence, under shadows.

"Stay still," Royce whispered, afraid to breath.

"I am," Frank hissed back, his voice quivering.

"ANYBODY OUT THERE?" The caretaker yelled again, sounding doubtful. It was quiet. The dog stopped barking, listening. The breeze rustled leaves in the treetops. A bat squeaked overhead. Then, only crickets. "I told ya it was just car brakes," the caretaker said to the dog. He slapped its butt and made it yelp, booting it back inside.

The door slammed.

"Not yet," Royce cautioned.

The white light went dark and Royce was up and over the fence in an instant. He and Frank gathered the paddles and life jackets and ran across the road, crashing down the embankment.

The dog was barking again.

"That was fucking close."

Toby and Will were waiting with the canoes in the water. Almost without breaking stride, Royce tossed Toby a paddle and threw the life jackets in the middle of the canoe. He pushed off and stepped into the back seat. Frank missed his footing and splashed into the river, but was out of the water and in the canoe quickly. Will pushed off from the bank and hopped in.

Heads down, they dug the paddles into the dark water, putting distance between themselves and the barking dog.

When the lights of the caretaker's house were but a tiny speck in dark clumps of shoreline trees, and the barking dog was far behind them, Toby called out to stop. Frank and Will glided up alongside. Everyone was breathing hard.

"I thought I was going to bust a gut...splash," Will gulped.

"Shut up," Frank said, angry.

"We're going to have a helluva time," Will was really winded, "taking these back tonight.

"What happened?" Royce asked.

"I fell in," Frank dejectedly said.

"Taking them back?" Toby said. "We're not taking these back tonight...not for awhile."

"What're you talking about?"

"I'm talking about Wisconsin. We're going to Wisconsin." Toby said. "We're going to the source of the Fox River. We're going to Green Bay."

They were paddling again, slowly upstream, in the middle of the dark river.

"Are you nuts?" Will protested. "I got to be back some time tonight, or my Dad'll skin me alive."

"Don't be such a femme, Will."

"Who you callin' a femme? Ya farmer."

"Wait a minute, Toby," Frank was trying to be reasonable. "This is crazy, like the time you wanted to steal a car in the middle of winter and drive it up the frozen river to McHenry."

"No. We're doing this."

It was silent a moment, just the sound of paddles.

"I'll go," Royce said firmly. "There's fucking nothing back there for me." He reached out and dug his paddle deep into the water as emphasis. The canoe veered left, but Toby corrected it.

"Hey ladies, you coming?" Toby called back.

"Shit," Will quietly swore.

"Wait up," Frank said.

And it was decided. They were going to the source of the Fox River. They were going to paddle all the way to Green Bay, Wisconsin.

{-5̆-}

They eased over the flat river, with tiny whirlpools trailing each paddle stroke, the canoes cutting gentle wakes, through the night and just on the fringe of a yellowish house and dockside lights. They stayed to the far left, skirting piers, on the lookout for boats, but especially wary of the sheriff's patrol boat.

At Haegar's Bend the river took a sharp, nearly 90 degree turn. The character of the river changed as dramatically as its direction. The water ran deep, cold, white capped and choppy. In a large powerboat the Bend was a sudden, bumpy turn, with one or two hull thumping jumps.

"Settle down," Royce called to Toby as the bow nodded up and came down hard.

"I am," Toby shouted back as the canoe rolled off a swell and splashed into a trough. "It's the Bend." He braced his legs under the seat as the canoe started rocking.

The river grew loud in their ears. Waves crashed against the stone breakwater on shore. Moored boats banged against rubber fenders. Metal clanged and rickety old docks cracked and creaked. The current was pushing them back. The canoe pitched up and down and threw spray all the way to the stern. A sudden wind whipped down on them from the side and the canoe nearly heeled over.

"I'm getting soaked."

A roller picked them up and carried the canoe sideways.

"Watch out for the dock!"

A black piling came straight at them. They narrowly missed it. A wave from the back slopped water into the canoe.

"Man, we're going to sink."

"We've got to power through." Toby called out.

"Right...dig...dig..."

Toby and Royce paddled into the white water, climbing swells, propelling the canoe down the backside. The front of the canoe was caught above water, in a hollow, and the fin of Royce's paddle slammed against the hull. His fingers were numb from the freezing water. Now they ached from slamming into the canoe. But he didn't stop paddling. He glanced to shore and saw they were making headway, slowly. A marker buoy with a red light bounced about wildly at the top of the Bend. That light didn't seem to be getting any closer. The river was getting rougher. Waves were coming in all directions. The canoe was being buffeted side to side, and crashing into rollers in front.

"Cross currents," Toby yelled out.

Royce wanted to yell back "no shit", but he was too busy paddling. Water was filling the canoe, sloshing at Royce's feet. He was sure they would founder. But there was the buoy, closer.

"We need to bail."

"Can't stop now," Toby said.

Frank and Will weren't far behind, battling the tricky currents of the Bend. Royce could make out Frank yelling at Will to steer and Will yelling back to shut up and paddle.

Suddenly the canoe slid off a large swell and listed hard over to the right. Royce grabbed the gunwale certain they were going over, but then he realized it was Toby in front pushing off the buoy, which was right next to them. Royce steadied himself and switched sides with the paddle.

And as quickly and as suddenly as the river had become wild with wind and cross currents, it smoothed out and resumed its slow, flat course. They were around the Bend.

They drifted forward, breathing hard, their hearts pounding, looking back as Will and Frank also fought their way past the buoy.

"My hair got wet," Toby said, irritated.

"I'm soaked."

Toby cupped his hands, bailing. Royce rubbed his hand and flexed his fingers, getting back feeling and some warmth.

Toby held up a dripping life jacket. "I thought you were nuts to take this, but I was ready to grab it if we tipped." He laughed, flinging a handful of water at Royce.

"Fucker!" Royce wiped the water from his face. "I thought we bought the farm."

"I ain't no farmer!" Toby shot back in mock anger.

They both laughed.

"If you'd just kept paddling instead of pissing your pants we wouldn't have almost sunk," Will was nagging at Frank.

"Well, if you knew how to steer we wouldn't have been zigzagging all over the river," Frank snapped back.

"Just keep paddling."

They bickered past Toby and Royce.

"Pipe down guys," Toby warned. "Somebody'll call the sheriff's patrol."

"He doesn't know how to paddle," Will grumbled.

"You don't know how to steer."

Each tried to get in the last word. Will stood halfway up, raising his paddle as if to clobber Frank. Frank saw him and started rocking the canoe. "Hey! Hey!" he cried out, laughing, falling backward almost out of the canoe. That make Frank laugh.

"C'mon...we've got to put some miles between us and Algonquin," Toby said.

They paddled upriver at an easy pace, four to five strokes then glide. The current was so slow they didn't need to exert themselves. Toby and Royce were quiet, each in his own thoughts. Royce was enjoying the river, the night, the calm, the freedom he felt being on his own. It was a funny sensation for him, to be completely involved in the moment with nothing dragging him down and nothing preventing him from going forward. Mostly, he had nothing to fear. Every once in awhile Toby would say something like "nice boat" or "look at that house" not so much to Royce as to himself. Royce was drying out from the drenching at the bend, which was good, because the night was gathering a chill. He felt the sweatshirt around his waist. It was also soaked.

Not far behind Frank and Will continued to bait each other. That was their way. They'd been friends since grade school and though at times it seemed like they had a strong dislike for the other, there was a strong bond between them. Royce thought it was because they were opposites. Will was big and loud, while Frank was below average height, skinny and more athletic. Frank was the good student and often had to tutor Will so he could get a passing grade. It was weeks before Royce learned Frank's nickname, which was Skip. He never found out why he was Skip, only that it was from grade school and he hated it. Will, on the other hand, was a junior and didn't like being called Willy or William. That was his father. Two things would make Will explode. Tease him about his complexion or call him Willy. Well, those were two things Royce knew for certain would set Will off. But it sometimes seemed Will didn't need any provocation to get his fists up.

"Cary," Toby offhandedly remarked, pointing to a cluster of lights ahead on the left side of the valley.

They were approaching a pair of bridges. The first, over Route 14 was a modern concrete bridge spanning the river. The high and slender pylons held the road bed high above the river. The second bridge was a dilapidated old wooden railroad trestle. It was an aged structure; all thick beams and cross supports, from another time. In the night, crossing the dark river, it looked spooky. It was a navigation hazard as the channel narrowed right through the center. You couldn't take a powerboat through either side, the water was shallow and supposedly filled with railroad junk, like a derailed box car.

"Why don't we catch a break?"

"On shore?" Royce asked.

"Under the bridge." Pilings surrounded the trestle, making a cluster with enough room for them to get out of the canoes. Royce grabbed onto a piling while Toby climbed past him, onto the cluster. It had the smell of tar and oil.

How're we going to keep the canoes from floating away?" Will said, bumping alongside Royce.

"Already figured that out," he answered. He pulled the belt from the wet life jacket and lashed the crossbars of both canoes together. "Give me the belt from the life jacket I gave you."

"What life jacket?" Frank replied.

"I took two and tossed you guys one."

Toby was inching his way around the trestle.

"Is that what I saw flying out of the canoe at the bend?" Will teased. "For a second I thought I lost ya."

"Shut up."

"Nevermind. I'll hold onto them." Royce jumped up to the pilings and sat with his legs dangling into the canoe, holding them against the slight pull of the river current.

"I'm cold. I'm tired," Will complained, leaning against the trestle. "But mostly, I'm hungry."

"You can eat me," Frank joked.

"You'd like that, ya 'mo." Will gave Frank a sharp jab in the shoulder. "No, I mean it. I'm really hungry."

"Well, Toby said, coming around the narrow edge of the piling. "There's a bunch of water rats on the other side. We could fry up a few."

"Mmmmmmm, fried rat."

"That's sick."

"If you were hungry enough, you'd eat'em."

"What? My shorts?"

"Shit. I wonder what time it is."

"Who cares."

"So tell me again this big plan to go all the way to Green Bay." There was just a hint of mockery in Will's voice.

"Don't be such a farmer," Toby said, sitting on the pilings. "That little thumb on Wisconsin? That's Green Bay—and my dad told me the Fox River starts there. I've been as far north as Grass Lake with my dad. He pointed out a wide channel and said it was the Fox and it went straight up through Wisconsin to Green Bay."

"I know the Fox empties into the Illinois River," Royce chimed in. "That goes into the Mississippi. We could've gone south, all the way to New Orleans."

"Yeah, but there's too many dams and spillways and long stretches of shallow water. Besides, barges go up and down the Illinois and we'd get swamped."

"Listen," Will held up his hand. "Sounds like water leaking."

"From the canoes?"

"It is leaking," Frank called out, standing at the end of the pilings. "I'm leaking."

"Don't shake it more than once, needle dick."

"Toby...Green Bay has to be a hundred miles away. This is crazy. It'd take us days to paddle there." Will was trying to persuade Toby against going.

"Aw, no way," Toby insisted, not to be dissuaded. "Two days...tops."

"We don't have any money. We don't have any food. Where're we going to sleep? It's getting cold."

"Did you guys notice Recharge is painted large and bright green letters on the side of the canoes?" Royce said.

"I got some money," Toby said.

"I've got a couple of bucks," Royce chipped in. "I got paid this week from Elektra's."

"Me too."

"Yeah," Will reluctantly said. "I do too...but we're not prepared for a long trip upriver."

"Not to worry," Toby confidently said. "The river will take care of us."

"What about curfew?"

"Frank? Grab the canoes. I've got to take a wiz."

"Sure, Royce."

"Well, I vote against it," Will said, holding his hand up.

Frank and Toby looked at Will. Nobody said a word. The only sounds were the gentle bumping of the canoes, a car going across the bridge overhead and Royce pissing in the river.

Will slowly lowered his hand. "Well, I guess we better get a move on," he sheepishly said, standing.

Algonquin

"I shook it three, four, five times...is that a sin?" Royce asked, hopping into the canoe. "Hope so. I was thinking of Mrs. Ruberg from English."

They laughed.

"With her tits out to here?"

"Sure you weren't thinking of old lady Elektra from work?"

That got another laugh. But not from Royce, telling them to "shut up."

"Why does that old lady like you, Royce?" Toby teased. "She's always touching your butt. I saw her, looking for a rise, but you're looking for a raise?"

"C'mon, Toby," Royce said, embarrassed.

They untied the canoes and paddled through the bridge and past Cary, toward Fox River Grove. The moon was setting. It was maybe very late at night, or maybe early the next morning. The houses on the banks were dark and shut for the night. There were few lights along the river.

"We're getting close to North Barrington," Toby said, noting the houses along the river were getting bigger and more opulent, and the piers had cabin cruisers at dock. "Find a good one."

"Good one?" Royce asked.

"A boat we can break into," Toby added. "Like that one." He pointed and Royce angled the canoe toward the stern of a very large cabin cruiser tied between two docks. What looked like a mansion was atop a sloping, well manicured lawn. It was shrouded in darkness except for a semi-circular row of tiny patio lights. "You break in," he told Royce. "There's got to be stuff we can use."

"What's up?" Frank whispered as they floated up.

"Shhhhh...don't bang the canoes."

The cruiser was zipped, snapped and buttoned up snugly with white canvas from the flying bridge to the stern. Royce jerked a corner of the canvas loose and wriggled inside. The dock light was shining inside, coming through the bridge Plexiglas, so he was able to make his way around the cabin in the half-light. It smelled musty inside. But it was a really nice boat—very expensive, with lacquered mahogany cabinets and polished brass fittings. He went through the cabinets and found a wide roll of silver duct tape and Swiss army knife. Down in the galley he grabbed a couple of cans in an upper cabinet and in the sleeping quarters found some shirts, sweatshirts, towels and a woolen army blanket. He bundled up the clothing and pushed it through the open corner.

"Food?" he heard Will hiss. "Did you find any food?"

Ransacking another cabinet he found a plastic water bottle, about half full, some loose change and a tiny can of something. Gathering this and the other cans, he handed it out to Toby. He paused a moment and looked around. He spied a length of rope and a small bucket. He handed these out the hole as well. Then he squirmed out the corner and back into the canoe.

"What're you doing?" Toby whispered.

"Snapping it back up."

"Food? Did you get any food?"

"Tidy little burglar, aren't you. Forget it," Toby chuckled under his breath. "Let's go."

They pushed off, paddling quietly and quickly away. Once around a bend in the river they slowed.

"What'd ya get?" Will asked anxiously. "Any food?"

"Here's a shirt."

"Awright. I was freezing."

"Give me one of those."

"And some water."

"Pass it around."

"Me first," Royce said, taking a swig and handing the bottle to Frank. "I was parched."

"Got some cans here." Toby held up each in the waning moonlight. "Sliced peaches...and Vienna sausages...and spam."

"We got food," Will said relieved. "But how're we going to open the cans."

"I got a Swiss army knife," Royce said, take the can of peaches from Toby. "You can have those sausages...I hate'em."

"More for me," Will said.

"Stow the towels and blankets where it's dry. Let's eat."

Royce knifed open the can of sausages and handed it to Toby, who took a couple and handed the can to Will. Opening the can of peaches Royce dug out two fingers and filled his mouth.

"I told ya the river would take care of us," Toby, chewing and taking the can of peaches from Royce, said.

They passed the cans back and forth, biting off hunks of greasy spam and gulping water from the bottle.

"I'll be ready for a good night's sleep after this," Will said, sounding happy again.

"We've got farther to go tonight," Toby said with his mouthful.

"Awwwww," Frank moaned. "My arms are aching."

"You call those pencils arms?"

"We've got to get past Barrington and closer to McHenry."

Will belched, and it resounded over the river.

Their hunger satisfied, and the chill dressed in stolen shirts and sweatshirts, it was now only their weariness that needed care. The lights from towns along the valley were becoming fewer and fewer as the darkness and the late hour consumed. Cars along the roads on the bank became more and more scarce. Houses were getting farther apart and all seemed dark for the night. There were shadows from trees and bushes overgrown all the way down to the riverbank. The sounds of their paddles seemed loud in the still and heavy air.

They were in a part of the river with few lights behind and no lights up ahead.

"Let's tie up here." Toby's voice was slow, tired. He turned the canoe toward a line of trees along the shore. It was a thickly wooded stretch with limbs hanging low over the water. Royce ducked as they floated underneath.

"Tie up to a limb."

Toby tied the bow of the canoe to a thick limb, while Frank tied up to a limb a little way down. Royce passed Toby a blanket and kept a large towel for himself. He handed two beach towels over to Frank for him and Will to use as blankets.

Awkwardly, Royce stretched out on the bottom of the canoe. The metal bottom was cold. He and Toby had enough room if they didn't try to lie on the same side. There was a small puddle of water in the middle of the canoe, but most of the water had been sopped up by the life jacket.

"We're real close to McHenry," Toby said with a yawn. "We could be through the locks early morning."

"You better stay on your end of the boat." Will warned.

"Shut up, ya femme."

Down in the bottom of the canoe Royce could hear the water lapping against it. There were crickets and noisy whirly bugs all around, yet it seemed peaceful. A train whistle sounded in the distance. He tucked his arm under his head and wrapped himself in the towel.

"It's 10PM," Will said trying to sound like a TV announcer. "Do you know where your children are?"

"Cram it Bozo," Toby shot back.

Someone farted and Frank laughed. Royce would've laughed also if he wasn't so exhausted.

{-6-}

A gentle rocking and the sound of water against the aluminum hull of the canoe woke Royce. A fly buzzed by. Birds were chirping. He struggled up on his elbow and peered over the gunwale. The sun was tipped on the horizon. He heard Toby snoring at the other end of the canoe; and Will and Frank in the other canoe.

A bouncing tree limb overhanging the river caught his attention. A large white bird, its head cocked to one side was staring at him with piercing yellow eyes.

Royce looked around and saw they were in a part of the river lined by pale aspen trees, and green cornfields as far beyond as he could see.

He had to take a piss.

There was a slight bend to the river and houses in the distance. He thought he knew where they were and they had got a lot closer to McHenry last night than he thought.

"What the hell time is it?" Will was saying.

"Shut up and go back to sleep," Frank sleepily replied.

They were stirring. At the front of the canoe Toby started and sat up. He massaged his face and saw Royce was awake.

"How long you been awake?" He yawned.

"Not long," Royce said. The noise disturbed the large white bird. It spread its wings and leaped off the limb, swooping low and flying across the river and into the cornfield.

"I gotta take a crap," Will complained.

"Well don't do it here?"

"We're pretty close to the McHenry locks," Toby said, sniffing and glancing upriver.

"What'd ya want me to do, hang my butt over the side?"

Frank laughed. "You do that and I'll push you in after your crap." They both laughed.

There was a clattering and bumping upfront and Royce glanced over to see Toby give him a grin and just lean over the side and plunge into the river. Frank and Will then scrambled up and jumped in. Royce didn't want to be the only one, so he pitched over the side as well.

The water was cold. The sun hot, and the river shallow enough they could stand. The brown water came up just over their waists.

"What're you doing?" Frank asked Will between laughing jags.

He was crouched low in the water and couldn't stop himself from laughing. Royce laughed also, peeing.

"I hope a fish comes up and bites your wiener off."

"Shut up...I'm...I'm concentrating." Will grunted.

"I'm getting out of here!" It isn't easy to get into a canoe from the river, but knowing Will was crapping in the river gave Royce an extra bit of energy to jump into the middle of the canoe. It tipped, but didn't take on any water. Once it settled Toby jumped in as well.

"Any of those towels dry?" he asked.

"This one. It's partly dry."

"Toby dried his face and hair. "Any food left?"

Royce looked into the bucket.

"Naw. We'll have to go into McHenry and get something to eat."

Will and Frank were fighting again, both trying to get back into the canoe at the same time. The canoe was tipping wildly and water was splashing all over.

"We should split them up?"

"You want to ride with one of them?" Toby asked, giving Royce a look.

"Now that you mention it...naw."

"Hey," Toby commanded. "Knock it off you two. We got to make time."

"Crap—just remembered," Royce said. He went into the bucket and pulled out the roll of duct tape. "Toby," he said, pulling off and tearing a long piece of tape. "...put this over the Recharge on the bow."

Toby took the length of tape. "Good idea. Hey Frank? Untie and move over here." He taped over the Recharge on the canoe; and then did the same on Will and Frank's canoe.

"Whose idea was that?" Frank asked.

"Royce's," Toby answered smoothing the tape over the green letters.

"Good idea," he said. "I guess all the girls are wrong," he added.

"What all girls?"

"I heard all the girls think Royce is good looking, but dumb."

"Eat me, Frank" Royce dryly retorted.

They paddled out into the middle of the river and started toward McHenry. It was very early morning, the sun rising on their right. No other boats were on the river.

Small summer cottages began to appear on either shore. Royce heard a truck then noticed a white van stopping at one of the cottages. A milkman jumped out the side door, ran to a cottage, the bottles clanging in a wire basket. He stopped paddling.

"Hey," Toby asked, turning. "Why'd you stopped paddling?"

"Let's turn into that dock."

"Why?" Then Toby saw the milkman hop back into this truck and drive a little ways down the road to another cottage. He saw the two bottles of milk on the front step by the door and understood.

They veered quickly into the dock.

"Hold the canoe," he said, stowing his paddle and leaping onto the pier. He ran at a crouch across the lawn and made footprints in the white dew on the grass. In one motion he snatched the milk bottles from the stoop and clutching the bottles to his belly, sprinted back to the pier and was in the canoe in minutes.

"Go," he breathlessly said. Royce was back paddling hard, then swung the bow around to the middle of the river and dug his paddle in. Once away from the pier he let the momentum glide the canoe upstream.

They were past a line of trees and out of sight of the cottage when Will and Frank came up alongside.

"What'd ya get?" Will asked.

"Thirsty?" Toby asked, proudly handing over one of the quarts of milk.

"Alright."

"Come on...keep paddling. Let's get away from here," Royce said.

Toby peeled off the paper cap and flung it into the river. He took a long drink and handed it back to Royce. The glass was cool, with beads of water running down the sides. Royce drank the cold milk and it tasted sweet and filling. They passed the bottle back and forth until it was empty. Then Toby threw it as far as he could toward the opposite shore. It landed with a splash, then bobbed up and floated downstream.

"That was cool," Toby was saying, taking up his paddle. "A surgical strike...like B-52s over Hanoi." With his voice, he made the sound of an explosion. "Wish we had some music...good music. " And he began to sing. "*Well everybody's heard about the bird, bird bird bird, the bird is a word...*"

They were paddling and laughing, with Frank and Will singing "*bird bird bird, the bird is a word.*"

"You hate that song, don'cha?" Toby said to Royce.

He shrugged. "It's okay."

"Okay? Okay? It's great. Not like the limey bands you like--The Beatles, Rolling Stones, The Booger Eaters and Turd Wingers. You should listen to American music not that English crap."

"I like it. I like the new stuff."

"Nobody will ever be better than Elvis. He's the king."

"Old Elvis," Royce said, sort of quietly.

"All that girly long hair is garbage."

An empty milk bottle tumbled through the air and caught sunlight as it flashed overhead and splashed alongside.

"Ya missed, Will!" Toby yelled back.

"I like American music, Martha and the Vandellas, Four Tops, Temptations, Smokey Robinson and the Miracles."

"Awwww, that's boogaloo music, not American, like The Beach Boys, Jan & Dean." Toby said. "So when you get a band together are you going to play that kind of stuff?"

"Yeah, some." Royce paused. "But I really want to play stuff by new bands like The Kinks or The Animals."

"Never heard of them," Toby said in a tone that signaled an end to the conversation.

"You guys shouldn't talk about music," Frank chimed in. "You'll just end up fighting."

They paddled in silence for a long time as the sun climbed higher in the morning sky, and the river widened.

Will was the first to spot the dam and locks ahead. He pointed and both canoes angled to the large concrete locks on the riverside. The river on the other side of the locks was a good ten to twelve feet above their heads. They drifted around the enormous concrete doors, half expecting them to automatically open. Finally, Toby yelled out to the lock master's office on top. "Hey? Anybody up there?"

There was no response.

The dam and locks were old, chipped and yellowing concrete, with rusted reddish metal bars. On the bottom corner of the enormous doors of the locks was etched 1907.

"Wake up!" Will added.

Still, there was no response.

"What're ya doing up there? Open the locks." All four were yelling.

"Drop your cock and open the lock," Will shouted, which made them break out in laughter.

At last the door creaked opened and a small bandy-legged white-haired man in a dingy off-white shirt and high-waisted pants held up by suspenders came out and peered over the railing.

"Whaddahya wan?" He seemed to be chewing something.

"Open the locks."

"Who fer? You fer? You two canoe? You ked me?" He had a thick eastern European accent. He spit something into the water and wiped his mouth with the back of his hand.

"We're not keeeeeeedding," Toby said. "Open the locks."

"Ahhhh, you go-un take ah hike...en I mean it. Dere's a path oveh dere." He pointed, turned, waved his hand in dismissal and closed the door.

"What's he mean?" Frank asked.

"It's called portage, guys," Royce said.

"And we're walking," Toby put in.

They paddled to the steep bank and a narrow muddy path up a grassy incline. It was slippery and they ended up dragging and banging the canoes behind. There was a parking lot at the top of the embankment, with a small park. They carried the canoes across the parking lot and past the locks. After the locks there was a boat launch. They carried the canoes down the long decline to the water's edge.

"If I had a free hand I'd flip off that old fart," Will said grappling with the canoe.

"Let's moon him," Frank suggested.

"Naw...let's just get going." Toby said.

"Yeah," Royce agreed. "We still got a long way to go yet."

"If we're going to get the Chain O' Lakes by tonight," Toby said, finishing Royce's thought.

They pushed off into the river and paddled into McHenry.

McHenry, an old town, looked a lot like Algonquin but noticeably more middleclass with upscale stores and mock Tudor designed restaurants and plain front taverns with a marina full of white-hulled cabin cruisers. They paddled past, looking at the people bustling about in the early morning, driving to work, shopping, caught up in the urgency of their own day-to-day lives.

"My dad's probably tightening the knot on his tie, gulping the last of the coffee from a cup, puffing a cigarette, smoothing the few strands of hair left on his head, grabbing his suit jacket and getting in the car to go to work," Royce said.

"My dad is already at work, in the machine shop, yelling at somebody for screwing up," Toby added. "Will? What's your dad doing right now?"

"Cussing me," Will said, half joking. "Well, about now he's driving into his job...engineer, with Western Engineering in Chicago. Probably listening to the news station, or the crappy polka music his likes."

"My dad is getting ready to go to his office in Elgin," Frank put in. "He'll be finishing his soft boiled egg, toast and tea. Same damn stuff he eats each and every morning since I can remember. Kissing my mom goodbye. Then he'll drive to his dad's factory, where they make toasters and heaters and this flange and that widget. Same damn stuff they've been making since I can remember."

"I'm not really looking forward to that," Royce said. "I want to do things. I want go places. I don't want anybody telling me when I have to get up, do this or do that."

"My dad would have a heart attack if I said something like that to him," Toby added. "He lectures me practically every day, that I have to get good grades in school, go to a good college, get a good job. Marry a good girl. Buy a good house. Have kids that are good."

Will laughed. "At least he's pushing you to have good stuff. My dad is constantly telling me that if I don't shape up I'll never amount to anything. I have to use my head—if I can pull it out of my butt."

"Ha!" Frank chuckled. "I think your dad's right."

"Shut up. What's your dad say to you?"

"Pretty much the same that Toby's dad says to him. Get good grades, go to college, marry, settle down, buy a house," Frank said with a shrug.

"What about you, Royce?" Toby asked. "What does your dad tell you to do?"

Royce was quiet a moment, uncomfortable. He took a breath, then said, "Nothing. He doesn't say anything about how he wants me to grow up. I don't think he gives a damn."

"Oh, C'mon," Will said. "He's got to care."

"No. I knew a long time ago I was a big disappointment to him." Royce stopped paddling and glanced away toward the shore. "Funny thing is I don't know what I did to make him feel that way. He never came to any of my little league games. He never went to any school functions. He never took me anywhere. It was never just a dad and his son."

The others were silent awhile. Finally Frank spoke up. "Sorry, guy. Sounds tough."

"I'm not sorry," Royce quickly said with some anger. "He disappointed me also."

"Now, my dad," Toby interrupted, maybe on purpose. "He pisses me off with the way he treats my ma. He treats her like a slave, get this, do that, clean the house, all the time."

"Yeah, I know what you mean," Will jumped in. "My dad says really mean things to my mom sometimes. She runs into the bedroom crying."

"At least he doesn't beat her," Royce said.

They became quiet again, until Frank broke the silence.

"Well, my dad is totally boring. He wants me and my sister to play cards with him, all the time. Or board games. Or let's go down to the gas station and fill the car then take a drive out in the country. How's school? Anything I can help you with? Drives me nuts."

They crossed under the Highway 120 overpass and could hear the commuter cars rushing overhead. The valley walls were less steep and farmlands rolled away from the shore, neat rows of tall green-brown corn ready for the combine, bunches of squat deep green soybeans, waving fields of yellow grain. There were fishermen on the banks, with lines far out into the river. One fisherman was wearing rubber waders and was standing waist deep in water off shore. They both waved to the boys as they paddled past.

{-7-}

North of McHenry the river and valley seemed restored to its more natural state, with few cottages, no towns, farmland mostly and conservation sites. They paddled along tree-lined banks, startling small clusters of sleeping ducks that flapped their wings wildly and quacked loudly as they took to the air. There was a constant drone of summer insects. Lazy cows eyed them silently as they passed; while fish leapt here and there.

"This is so cool," Toby said. "Like we're the first explorers paddling up an unknown river."

It was that cool, like no other people, except Native Americans, had come this way before. With a kind of awe they paddled upriver.

But then the modern world would interrupt every so often and a powerboat would overtake them. They would get a wave from the driver as they turned into the boat's wake.

The day grew hot, then hotter and to cool off they would dive in, then scramble back into the canoe. Drying off took only a few minutes. Toby had his shirt off, as did Will. Royce was self-conscious and wouldn't take his off. Frank was complaining he was cold. That set Will off, saying he had to always be contrary.

Around a bend roared a ski boat speeding toward them. The driver was looking back at the water skier and didn't turn to see the canoes until the skier started waving his hand.

"What's he doing?" Royce said with alarm.

The boat was nearly on them, but veered off at the last second. However, the grinning water skier was out for some sport and bore down on them.

"Duck!" Toby yelled.

The water skier leaned at the last moment, cutting a long and tall rooster tail of spray that drenched them.

"A-hole!" Will screamed. "You A-hole!"

Frank flipped the bird to the water skier, who was laughing with his middle finger up also.

Then the boat wake hit them like storm surf, tossing the canoes about.

"C'mon back here ya 'mo" Will was raging.

"I was hot anyway," Toby said, chuckling.

"Yeah," Royce replied, wiping the water from his face, and tossing his hair back. "Me too." The wake hit the shore, loud like ocean waves.

The day went along, paddling up the river with green bushes and trees tilted over the shoreline. Clouds of noisy birds flew crazy eights in and out of the treetops. A few signs of people showed, a dilapidated gray wood pier, missing boards and no longer attached to the bank. A duck blind or fishing hut, some gravel roads or blacktop overgrown with tall weeds and going to nowhere; though mostly the river appeared pristine.

"I'm getting hungry," Will reminded anyone within earshot.

"Next town," Royce said. "We'll stop and get something to eat."

"That may be a long time," Toby said in a low tone.

"I know," Royce responded, "But I don't want him to know that."

"It's been a hard night's day," Will was singing, off-key and in a cracking voice. *"And I've been paddling like a dog."* He and Frank broke up in laughter.

"Is that really true what you said about your dad?" Toby asked.

"What? That he doesn't give a crap about me?"

"No," Toby was serious. "That he beat your mom?"

Royce thought a long time, realizing he should never have said something like that. He should've kept his walls up. No one else would understand.

"I mean, you don't have to tell me or nothing." Toby was saying quickly, to cover his asking. "We've heard them yelling at each other before."

"No. No," Royce replied. "It's okay. Yeah, he beat her. Broke her arm once. Black eyes and punching and all that...all the time."

"Wow, I would never have thought your dad would do stuff like that. I mean, isn't he like an executive and didn't he go to some big time school in the east?"

It was the drinking, but Royce would never tell anyone that. He had already said too much.

"Yeah, Ivy League," Royce answered.

"Does he beat her a lot?" Toby seemed curious, and sounded genuinely sympathetic. It made Royce lower his guard.

"Not so much anymore."

"Not so much? Did he stop?" Toby asked.

Royce took a breath. Did he dare confess something about the private horrors of his home life? The weight might be less to carry.

"A couple of years ago," Royce found himself saying. "He was pushing my mother around...they were both," he stopped. He couldn't say it. "They were both real tired and he was slapping her. She was crying and he was yelling he was going to shut her up for good."

"Holy crap," Toby was shocked. "Where were you?"

"I was sleeping and woke up. I went into the room and..." his voice trailed off. In his mind he was reliving that night.

"Then what?"

Royce did not want to go on, but knew Toby would pester him until he finished the story. "Then, he wasn't in front of me anymore, and not slapping my mother."

"Was he pissed at you?"

"No," Royce said with a hint of shame.

"Did you clobber him? I don't think I ever saw you just haul off and punch out anybody. I didn't think you were like that."

"A guy's dad is supposed to be the person you look up to...the guy you want to grow up to be," Royce was saying to no one and almost in anger.

"So he doesn't slap her around anymore, huh?" Toby asked after awhile.

"Nope," Royce said, ashamed. "He'll start yelling and I'll open the door and tell him to shut up and he'll glare at me...but he stops."

"Wow, you told your dad to shut up? Parents are weird," Toby added.

"Adults are fucked up," Royce said with punctuation.

"My dad..." Toby said in a hushed voice. "He doesn't hit my ma or anything like that. But he does treat her like dirt. Get me my cigarettes." He said in a mocking tone. "Where's my beer? Make me a sandwich. She works all day long cleaning the house and taking care of my brother. He just doesn't give her a break. It makes me mad sometimes."

Will was calling loudly from behind.

"Are we there yet?" he repeated over and over.

"A little further upriver and we'll be in the Chain O' Lakes," Toby yelled back. "We better step on it," he added to Royce. They dug their paddles into the brown river and picked up the pace.

"Hey, wait up," Frank could be heard saying as he and Will started to fall back.

{-8-}

Though the afternoon was drawing late, the sky on the horizon was light blue ahead. A wind was kicking up, rustling late summer leaves and bending the trees on the shoreline. They had to stay over to the edge of the channel, as more and more boats were going up and down the river.

Then, almost without noticing, they were under a highway bridge and in a lake.

"That's it," Will said. "Chain O' Lakes."

"It's not," Toby yelled back, over the roar of a passing powerboat. "But we're close."

The lake opened before them and spread over a large area. The wind blew stronger, and the water started to chop.

"We should stay near the bank," Royce said.

There were expensive houses along the shore, all with sand beaches and piers. Power and sail boats were scattered around the lake. After the narrow confines of the river they felt dwarfed. The on water activity itself had them looking all around.

Ahead loomed the tall columns and high arching roadbed of the Highway 12 Bridge. The town of Fox Lake was to their right, a bustling suburb with afternoon traffic teeming over its streets and roadways.

"Look at the size of that bridge," Will said, looking up in awe.

"Ever been up river this far?" Toby asked Royce.

"Nope," he replied, also marveling at the high bridge. "Never."

They were hugging the right shoreline, sheltered from the wind, but having to battle cross wakes from the boats. Still, they paddled hard and slipped under the bridge. Narrows connected this lake to the next.

"Fox Lake," Toby said, pointing toward the end of the narrows.

Fox Lake was the largest of the Chain O' Lakes, and the busiest and most populated. The town of Fox Lake was spread out on either shore, houses, marinas, boats, swimming areas surrounded them. Buoys with blinking red lights and tall wood pilings marked the channels and open waters for boats.

Toby stopped paddling, turned around and laid his paddle across the canoe. He leaned on the paddle, with his head down.

"What's up?" Royce asked.

"Man," he said with a big breath. "We've done some miles...and I am really hungry."

"There ya go," Will agreed, as their canoe slipped alongside.

"Okay," Royce said. "We can stop..." and he waved his hand around "...just about anywhere."

"Well," Toby started, "we have to cross over to the left shore, and stay on the left shore to pick up the Fox River after Grass Lake. But we can stop at the Grass Lake bridge."

"Can ya hold out Will?" Frank asked.

"I'm skin n'bones," he said, pinching a small roll of fat on his belly. "Just skin n'bones. But...I guess..." he shrugged and said, "if I have to wait...I'll survive a little longer."

They all laughed. Toby took up his paddle and spun forward.

"Just barely," Will added.

Dusk was falling, the sky softening, and stars began to dot the deepening blue. Over to the west the top arc of the red sun was falling down a far jagged horizon. Lights from the town of Fox Lake came on, first street lights, then house lights, the colorful blaze of businesses in neon. Boats were heading into dock, white stern lights, red and green bow lights clustering close to shore. The wind slacked off to an occasional breeze as the cool of the water and the air evened the temperature.

It was easier to paddle as the water seemed heavier and every stroke took them far forward. Up ahead, the low, old wood, Grass Lake road bridge drew nearer stroke upon stroke. And with each stroke dusk gave way to night.

Passing under the Grass Lake bridge they went through shadows and left the light and noise of Fox Lake far behind.

A marina and adjacent park was up ahead, and what looked like a carnival, with a Ferris wheel and Tilt-A-Whirl with a chaos of colored lights and the music of a calliope.

"Hey, let's stop there," Will shouted.

"Okay," Toby said, angling the bow of the canoe toward shore.

"We can put the canoes in the reeds over there." Royce pointed to a clump of reeds, bushes and seedlings just at the end of the parking area. It was a muddy shore, but they put in and dragged the canoes up into the undergrowth. They hunched low under branches and came out of the reeds to the parking area. Scattered cars and trucks were parked in rows, but closer to the carnival on the other side of the lot.

"How do I look?" Will asked, ducking into his T-shirt.

Night was full now, a half moon overhead, but like moths they were drawn to the brightness, the hurly burly and the sounds of the carnival. Toby and Royce started across the parking area. Frank and Will smoothed out their hair and clothes and ran to catch up.

Smoke billowed around a dirty-white trailer in the corner of the parking area. There were black smudges above the small windows.

"Smell that? Smell that?" Will asked excited. "Let's get some burgers. I'm dying of hunger." They were all hungry, so it didn't take much persuading from Will. Quickly they crossed the parking lot and lined up, waiting to step forward to the eye level window and order food.

Royce checked the prices on a placard. "A dollar fifty for a cheeseburger?" he grumbled. "That's a lot."

"Yeah, a quarter for a coke and fifty cents for fries," Toby added, also studying the prices.

Will was first at the order window, which was about chin high to him. A shadowy figure inside, leaned down.

"Whud'll it be, kid?" a bored voice drawled.

"A cheeseburger, a coke and fries," Will said.

"Two dollah, thurdy-eight," the voice said.

Will dug out wet bills from his pocket, and carefully peeled apart the ones stuck together. A dirty hand with a blue tattoo snatched the bills.

"Jesus," the inside voice said. "Wha'cha been doing, kid, swimming in duh river?"

"Kinda," Will replied, leaning back and smirking at Frank.

"Ah'll have ya order up in a minute," and the dirty hand spilled change into Will's palm. A Coke in a paper cup with a straw, slid out the window.

Frank stepped up as Will sidestepped from the window. He ordered a cheeseburger, fries and a Coke, and had his money ready. Behind him Toby and Royce were picking out wet bills and getting ready to order. In the end all four ordered the same, cheeseburger, fries and a Coke. They went over to an unvarnished picnic table and sat drinking their Cokes.

Toby picked up a flyer from the table. He wiped ketchup off it and held it up to the light.

"Royce? Ever heard of The Frantic?" He asked.

Will let out a burp and breathy sigh.

"The Frantic? Yeah, I think I have. Why?" he asked, taking the straw from his mouth.

Frank took a long, loud drink.

"They're playing tonight," Toby said, the straw in his teeth. "So is some big guy named Baby Huey.

"Baby Huey and the Babysitters...here? Cool."

"Yeah," Toby said. He handed the flyer to Royce. There was a picture of five guys about Royce's age. They were dressed in dark turtle necks and jackets standing sideways and in a rigid pose, behind the blot of what was ketchup.

"Cheeseburger fries, cheeseburger fries," the voice called from the window.

"That's us," Frank said, jumping up, with Will at his heels. He took the red checkered paper baskets from the window, handing one back to Will. "Ketchup?"

"Side shelf," the voice replied.

As Will and Frank piled their cheeseburgers with pickles, puddles of ketchup and mustard, onions, the voice in the white van called out, "cheeseburger fries, cheeseburger fries."

"And that's us," Toby said, climbing out of the picnic bench. Royce followed, taking his paper basket from the hand out the window. It was a good mound of crinkle cut fries, but a smallish cheeseburger. Royce didn't care, he was hungry.

They sat around the picnic table eating hurriedly and in silence, except for the occasional smack and slurp and straw pulling at the bottom of the empty Coke cup. Will finished first, with a loud exhale.

"Oh, man, I was starving," he said, slapping his stomach. "What's that?" he said to Frank, pointing to the right. Frank looked and Will stole a fry from Frank's basket.

"Hey!" Frank protested. Will just laughed.

They finished quickly, shaking the ice at the bottom of the cups and trading belches. Will topped them all, longest and loudest. It drew some disparaging glances from people lined up at the van window.

"Can't take you anywhere," Toby joked.

Fed, they lazed around the picnic table.

"What're we going to do now?" Frank asked after awhile.

"I dunno," Toby said.

"Let's see what's here," Royce suggested.

"You want to go see that band?" Will asked.

"Yeah, that would be cool," Royce answered.

"Okay!" Toby slapped his knees, stood, stretched, then said, "if I don't do something now, I'm going to fall asleep. C'mon, let's go."

Standing, dropping the empty, crumpled, greasy bottom paper baskets in a large green drum, they walked toward the rows of lights and carnival rides. It was a standard variety of traveling carnival, with the usual rides--a small roller coaster called The Mouse; a pendulum ride, Ferris Wheel and a merry-go-round. There was a clown in a dunk tank and games of skill and chance. Girls screamed as the Tilt-A-Whirl spun by.

"Hey Ya! Hey Ya! Win a Teddy Bear..."

"Three spins a quarter!"

It smelled of sawdust, mildew, diesel and axle grease. People with pink cotton candy ambled past. Popcorn popped and the stink of a cigar drifted by.

"Maybe we can find a fortune teller," Will said. "Oh Swami, will Frank get laid this summer?" They snickered and Will got a shove from Frank. "Shut up!"

"Four balls a quarter. Win a prize!"

"Toby?" Will stopped and grabbed Toby's elbow. "You could win this game." It was a pyramid of silver painted wooden milk bottles.

"It's rigged," Royce warned, but no one was listening.

Toby stopped and watched a middle-aged man rear back and hurl a baseball at the bottles. A little girl was standing beside him with big eyes on the stuffed animals and other colorful prizes decorating the walls. One—miss. Two—miss. Three—miss. And he missed with his fourth throw.

"Awww, tough luck," a short lady behind the counter said. She wore a stained white apron. "Try again. C'mon, don't be shy."

But the middle-aged man just shook his head and took the hand of the disappointed little girl.

"How 'bout you boys," the short woman barked out, holding four balls in one hand and motioning for Toby and Royce to step forward. "Four balls a quarter. Win a prize."

"I will if you will," Toby said, trading a glance at Royce.

"Yeah, alright," Royce replied.

They stepped forward, each pulling a quarter out of their pockets and slapping them on the counter. The woman got closer and Royce almost started when he saw her up close. She deftly scooped both quarters off the counter and set four balls in front of Royce, and four in front of Toby.

"Knock'em all down and you win a panda. Three bottles a bear; two bottles pick a prize. Let'er fly boys!" She backed off to the side.

Toby took a step back, and went into a full windup and threw. The ball went high and thumped behind the bottles. Royce did the same, with a windup, aiming at the base of the bottles. His first ball bounced off to the side. Toby let up a bit on his second throw, which went off to the left. Thump! Royce's second was high. Thump!

"Shit," Toby hissed. His eyes narrowed and he threw, knocking the top bottle off.

"Atta boy! One more and you win a prize," the lady said, then called out, "Hey, we gotta winner here!"

Royce's third ball went wide right, and he quickly chucked his last ball, missing all the bottles. Toby though, was determined to win. He went back to a full windup. The ball hit the side of a wooden bottle. It tipped, teetered, rocked, but did not fall.

"Awwww, tough luck," the lady said, putting the top bottle on the stack. "How 'bout 'nother go. You were that close, Bucko!"

"I hit it," Toby was saying. "I hit it." He was pissed off. "Yeah," and slapped another quarter harder to the counter. "I'm gonna win this," he said as an aside to Will and Frank. They glanced at each other.

"How 'bout you, Sonny?" the lady said to Royce, four balls in her hand.

"Naw," Royce responded, backing off, trying not to stare at the carnival lady. She was old, with a coned head and hairline way up the crown of her forehead. Her features were narrow with a twisted mouth. He'd seen people with similar features and he suddenly felt sorry for her, realizing she was probably a forceps baby. He watched her, trying not to be obvious, but it fascinated him

Toby's first ball thumped the back wall, rocking the bottles, but not upsetting them. His teeth clenched and he cussed with each miss. When he ran out of balls, he dug into his pocket for another quarter.

"Grab him," Royce called to Will and Frank.

"Hey," he protested, "I'm gonna win this damn game."

"No, you aren't," Royce said, as they pulled him away.

"C'mon back," the lady was barking. "You're a winner. A winner!"

"You can't win," Royce explained. "They have the bottles on fishing line, or weighted. There's no way."

Toby calmed down, then after a moment exhaled and spat.

"Let's go see that band," Will suggested.

"Maybe there'll be some chicks?" Frank offered hopefully.

"Now you're talking," Toby said, clapping his hands together. "We're on Beaver Patrol, boys."

"Alright!" Will and Royce echoed.

They weaved through the straw strewn alleys of the carnival, with lighted games, rides and families walking about. Calliope music swirled from the merry-go-round, with little kids clutching their mother's dress, crying in fear as brightly painted wild-eyed sparkle horses with grotesque expressions whirled by. Lights flashed and blinked, as barkers called out. There was laughter, shouts and excitement. A band was tuning up on a lighted stage across a short square of grass. People in groups were scattered here and there. Red embers from cigarettes glowed in the darkness, followed by clouds of gray smoke. The four walked down the middle of the open grass, close to the stage front.

"Anybody you know?" Toby asked Royce.

"Yeah, I've seen the drummer and singer at a music store in Dundee," he replied.

Tuned and trading looks of 'you ready?' the singer stepped up to the microphone, getting a squeal of feedback right away. He was short and stocky, dressed in what seemed to be the same turtleneck sweater and jacket as the photo on the flyer. All the members of the band were dressed like that. They had the popular equipment; Vox Amps and PA, a Fender Reverb and the bass player had a knockoff Hofner violin bass guitar.

"Test...test," the singer recited into the microphone.

Every member of the band had their hair combed forward trying for a rebellious fringe look.

"We're The Frantic and..." the singer paused, not sure what to say next. He laughed, finishing with "we're gonna play some tunes."

The drummer counted down and the band started into *Little Latin Lupe Lu.*

" *Wanna tell ya 'bout my baby...* "

Royce was watching the drummer, while slapping his hands on the sides of his cut-offs in time and nodding his head.

"She's my high flyin' baby..."

The drummer had a loose snare which Royce didn't like. He could hear the buzz from the low notes on the bass guitar vibrating the snares on the bottom head of the drum. He liked a tight snare, one that would crack with the flick of his drum stick. The drummer also used a French grip on his sticks, while Royce preferred an overhand grip. He probably did it for the bounce. His kit was a Slingerland, dark wood, single tom tom, with a floor tom. He had a small crash cymbal, and large ride cymbal, with a standard high-hat. His bass drum was large, and it had a soft resonating boom. Royce liked a smaller bass drum, with a sharp thud. But he was a good drummer, always on beat. He wasn't fancy, sticking to three-four and four-four rhythm.

"Little Latin Lupe Lu..."

"They any good?" Frank loudly asked into Royce's ear.

"Yeah. They're alright." Royce didn't want to say that he was jealous and would've liked to be up there himself, playing.

A crowd was starting to gather, teenagers gravitating to the stage and the music. Girls were dancing together or standing in groups looking around. Guys were hanging back, also in groups, trying to seem cool and disinterested while casting sideways looks at the girls.

The Frantic went from *Little Latin Lupe Lu* on beat into *Jolly Green Giant,* breaking only for the singer to say

"From the Valley of the Jolly...ho ho ho..." It impressed Royce.

"Look at those girls," Toby was saying to Will and Frank, giving Royce a nudge.

A group of five or six girls were all standing off to the side of the stage, bobbing to the music. A couple had teased and ratted and sprayed up bouffant hairdos. Others had shoulder length straight hair with bangs, which was more of a contemporary look. They wore tight jeans, white and multi-colored blouses, with bare midriffs.

"Let's..." Royce started to say, and was about to finish "go over and talk to them," but Toby, with Frank and Will trailing, was already on his way. Royce followed.

They got close and the girls noticed them, turning and becoming quiet and eying them.

"Hi," Toby said. "Me and my buddies were just wondering why cute girls like you didn't have dates."

The girls laughed, in a flattered sort of way. It was an ice-breaker, something Toby was good at, and it did the trick.

"We were waiting for you guys," a tall girl, who had her eye on Toby, replied with a hint of sarcasm.

"Well, here we are. I'm Toby. This is Royce," Toby pointed his thumb toward Royce. "And this is Frank and Will."

All traded a "hi," some shy, some with interest. One petite girl, with a gentle smile, said a soft "hi" to Royce and then dropped her eyes. The sound of her voice sparked something in Royce. "What's your name?" he asked her.

She was surprised by his attention, and with eyes looking up at him, then down to the ground, she hesitantly replied, "Shelly."

The tall girl was Donna and she and Toby paired off and went out into the crowd of dancers.

Shelly looked after them and Royce caught it, asking, "you want to dance too?" He held out his hand. Shelly smiled, placing her hand in his and letting him lead her into the group of dancers.

The Frantic were playing *Night Train* and it was easy to dance to. Toby caught sight of Royce and Shelly and arched his eyebrows, grinning at Royce.

Royce and Shelly stayed out for a couple of dances, then went back to the others. Shelly was laughing at Royce who was saying he never danced before and wasn't very good at it. She couldn't have been more than five feet tall, with a small cute face and big brown eyes. There was a reddish tint to her hair. Royce couldn't help himself and looked at her trim figure, with small breasts and round little butt.

Frank and Will were talking to the other girls in the group, telling jokes, and making them laugh. Royce and Shelly drifted off to the side. She went to Grant High School and was going to be a sophomore when school started in September.

"You guys aren't from Grant, are you?"

"Is it that obvious?"

"Cut-offs, surfer shirts, guys from Fox Lake don't dress like that," she said.

"We're from Algonquin," Royce replied.

"Algonquin?" Shelly exclaimed. "That's way far. What're you doing here?"

"We got lost on our way to Lake Geneva," Royce joked, pausing as Shelly looked at him skeptically, then added. "It's a long story."

"All you Algonquin guys Rah-Rahs?"

"Rah-Rahs?" Royce said aloud with a laugh. "Not me...not us."

"You got that kinda long hair," Shelly teased, reaching up and slowly pushing his hair behind his ear.

"I play music."

Shelly's eyes lit up. "Yeah? What do you play?"

"Drums."

Her hand fell gently from his hair to his arm, lightly touching him. Royce was close to her with his hand touching her bare midriff.

"That's cool. Are you in a band? I'd come see you play."

"No, not yet...and really, I'm just starting out."

"What kind of music do you like?"

"Beatles mostly and Motown..."

Shelly took in a breath. "I love Motown and the soul stuff." She leaned close. Royce could smell her perfume. He could feel her warmth. "I really like The Beatles too," she whispered. "But don't tell Donna. They don't like longhair on guys."

There was a commotion in the shadowy mass of dancers. Both Royce and Shelly looked up. Toby and Donna were surrounded by a bunch of guys. Right away Royce noticed the greased back hair and he knew it was trouble. They were hoods.

"You gotta go!" Shelly said to Royce. "You gotta go right now!"

"What's going on?" Royce was confused.

"Those are Round Lake guys. They're gonna kick your ass."

Will was standing next to Toby, facing a gang of guys. Royce started for Toby and Will.

"Royce...wait!" Shelly grabbed his hand and uncapped a ballpoint pen. "Call me." She said, writing on his palm.

The voices were getting louder over the music.

"We were just dancing," Toby was saying.

"Don't forget...call me." And Shelly disappeared.

Royce came up alongside Toby. The biggest guy saw him. "Another Rah-Rah. C'mon, we're gonna kick your ass too."

Donna had switched sides and was standing next to the big guy. Royce saw Shelly come up behind another member of the hoods. He looked at her and she glanced away. Shelly's guy looked from Royce to Shelly. "You looking at my girl, shithead?" He was short, with wavy hair and cigarette behind his ear. "Hey! I'm talking to you!"

Royce was getting a quivering in his belly, with a dry mouth and his chest tight. "Ye-Yeah, why?" he said, trying to sound tough, but failing.

"Ha!" Shelly's guy laughed. "Listen to the 'tard ye-ye-yeah. All of the hoods laughed.

'Shut up!" Will yelled. He moved forward, with a mean look in his eye.

"Nobody's talking to you, pizza face!"

It was a tense moment, as Shelly's guy glared at Royce.

"Stomp his ass into mud, Kev," someone in the gang said.

"We're going," Toby suddenly said, his hands up and palms open, starting to back away.

"Not before we kick your ass," the big guy said. "C'mon chicken...let's go"

Kev took a step toward Royce. Shelly reached out and grabbed his arm to hold him back, but he jerked it away. "Sc-sc-scared?"

"No way...we're going."

He swung wildly at Royce, missing him as Royce leaned back.

"Let's go!"

Toby and Royce wheeled, pulling at Will, and took off running, dodging through the dancers. The hoods followed, close on their heels. They ducked and shoved their way through the crowd on the midway and reached the parking lot. Looking back, the gang was still coming after them. People in the crowd stopped and looked.

The Frantic were singing "*Na...Na Na Na Na...Na Na Na Na...Na Na Na...Na Na Na...*"

They ran across the dark parking lot. A bottle crashed against the bumper of a parked car and glass flew behind them.

"*You gotta know how to pony...*"

"Look at the little girls run." And the hoods laughed.

"*Like Bonie Maroni...*"

They reached the canoes, breathless. Frank was there and he had the canoes upright and ready to push off into the river.

"Mashed potato...do the alligator..."

"I could've taken that guy," Will said as they paddled out into the river. "He called me pizza face."

They were back out in the lake.

"Na...Na Na Na Na...Na Na Na Na..." The Frantic sang, way back on shore.

"I don't think I could've taken that big guy," Toby said quietly to Royce.

"Yeah...I dunno if I could've taken the other guy, either," Royce responded.

"Hey, Frank," Will said. "Where were you?"

"I was there," Frank said hesitantly.

They paddled far from the bright lights of the carnival, north under a half moon.

"I didn't see you."

"I was behind you," Frank protested.

"Oh, behind me," Will teased Frank. "Great. This huge hood is going to beat me to a pulp and you're there for me."

Soon they were deep into the night, beyond the noise, lights and town. There was a large dark square shadow up ahead, in the rushes near the bank. Toby steered the canoe toward it.

"What's up there?" Royce asked.

It was an abandoned duck blind and Toby grabbed onto a piling next to it.

"We're in luck. We can sleep here tonight," he said. He clamored out of the canoe and into a door-like opening. It was about eight by eight feet, and rickety. Royce tied up the canoe and held Will and Frank's canoe as they climbed into the blind. He tied all the canoes to the piling, grabbed his sweatshirt and stepped inside. It swayed with every movement, but it didn't collapse. It didn't smell too bad and had a roof and a floor. Royce brushed aside empty beer cans, spread out some old newspapers and lay down, covering himself with his sweatshirt. He propped his head against a board along the wall.

"I'm tired," Frank said, yawning.

"Probably from hiding," Will replied, sleepily.

"Get some sleep," Toby said. "We can get an early start in the morning."

"I was there."

Royce couldn't sleep right away and he lay there thinking about Shelly. He liked her and thought she also liked him. He held his hand up, and in the pale light of the moon saw only smudged ink on his palm.

"Toby?" he whispered.

"Yeah?"

"You liked that Donna, didn't you?"

"Yeah...I got a couple of feels. She was kinda hot. Your redhead was cute," he said.

"We should've..."

"We would've," Toby interrupted, "got our asses stomped, Royce. Forget it. Go to sleep."

"Yeah...I guess you're right," Royce said. He thought about Shelly a long time and wondered if he would find her again.

{-9-}

Morning sun flashed through gaps in the slates of the duck blind, catching Royce in the eyes and making him wince and turn away. He could hear the lake lapping against the pilings just below the floorboards. Ducks quacked and birds chirped and somewhere on the lake a motorboat started up.

Will was snoring.

"Toby?" Frank whispered. There was no response. "Toby?"

"Yeah, Frank," Toby mumbled.

"Don't you think we should head back now? My parents are probably going nuts."

It was quiet a moment.

"No, Frank," Toby replied, rising up on his elbows. "We are way more than halfway there."

"We're not even in Wisconsin yet," Frank protested in a harsh whisper.

Royce sat up, yawning.

"We're about an hour, at the most, from the Wisconsin border," Toby said. He stood and the whole duck blind creaked as if about to tumble into the lake. "Crap," he said, steadying himself. "Be easy when you get up."

Frank exhaled sharply, resigned.

Royce glanced at his palm and the faded blue smudge, feeling disappointed. Shelly was cute and fun. They had a spark and he would've liked to see her again.

Carefully, so not to bring the duck blind crashing down around them, they got into the canoes.

"Should we wake Will? Or just leave him?" Royce asked.

"I'll wake him," Frank replied. "Hey! Will!"

"Did you hear that guy?" Toby said quietly to Royce. "He wants to quit the mission when we're so close." He sounded disgusted.

"Yeah," Royce agreed, pushing off a piling, letting the canoe drift toward open water.

Frank, with Will groggily feeling his way out the duck blind and into the canoe, untied the bow and paddled through the rushes joining Royce and Toby on the lake.

The sun washed the sloping valley in a golden light. Wisps of white clouds, like strands of pulled cotton, spread across a pale blue sky. The lake was before them, in a morning peace. Glints of silver from sunlight caught the small waves. Down the shoreline they could make out the carnival breaking down and loading out. And in the distance, the town of Fox Lake was cast in long shadows.

"How're we going to find the river again?" Frank wondered aloud.

"Easy," Toby responded, annoyed at Frank asking. "We'll just stay to the left and follow the channel markers."

"You sure we're headed north?" Royce risked saying.

Toby looked over his shoulder with an expression like 'not you too?', but replied, "Yeah...my dad took our boat up here when I was younger. He pointed out the Fox River inlet, and it was to the left."

"C'mon Frank," Will was yelling. "Put your back into it. They're getting way ahead of us."

"Put your mouth on it...or I'll put your ass in the water." Frank snarled, sounding his disappointment about not turning for home.

"Whoa...I'm shaking," Will was laughing. "Now you're Mr. Tough Guy...not like last night when those hoods were after us."

"I was there," Frank protested.

"I didn't see ya. How come we met you at the canoes?"

"'Cause I'm fast and you're slow..." Frank shot back.

Toby and Royce led, following the contour of the left bank, just a few yards from the reeds. Frogs croaked and splashed into the still eddies along the lake shore. Ducks flew overhead. Behind, Will had shouldered his paddle and was taking aim. "Blam...Blam...Blam."

"Missed'em all," Frank said.

The sun was heating up the morning as they paddled through the flat brown water.

"What was your girl's name again?" Royce asked.

"From last night? Donna," Toby replied. "She was kinda slutty."

Royce laughed. "You weren't complaining." Toby added a nasty chuckle.

"I tell ya...if those hoods hadn't shown up..." and he trailed off.

"The girl I was with was named Shelly...and I gotta say...I liked her."

"You'd've liked to get in her panties..."

Thoughtfully, Royce replied, "yup."

Of the four Toby and Royce were considered the most experienced with girls. It was never asked, but Will and Frank didn't think Toby or Royce virgins. Their experience with girls was a lot less. This was for a variety of reasons, shyness and maybe just a lack of chances. Both Will and Frank would've given any sum of money, or half their college funds, to get laid just once. Any conversation about girls and sex would have Will and Frank listening, uncomfortably silent.

Toby claimed to have lost his virginity over Christmas break, in the back of a station wagon with a girl from his neighborhood. Who she was, or intimate details...he wouldn't divulge.

Royce said he lost his cherry to a girl, 17 years old from Elgin. That raised doubting eyebrows, as if he was making it up. But he wasn't. He and the girl from Elgin would go out at night, walk around, talk, listen to music on the transistor radio and end up in a wooded area. They would spread out their coats and lie down and make out. It started with her unbuttoning his jeans, while he pulled down her ski pants. She would jack him off, while he fingered her. Then one night she told Royce he could put it inside her, but just the tip, and no further. He had to promise. He promised, in a heartbeat. Her skirt was up and her panties down and Royce, shaking with excitement and fear, settled between her spread legs. "Just the tip," she reminded him sternly. He set the tip on her bushy lips. He could feel the warmth, and she was very wet. He gently pushed and was in. Instantly, he forgot his promise and thrust deep inside her. "Hey Hey Hey," she protested. "Don't you jizz in me," she yelled, beating on his chest. He couldn't stop himself and went in and out rapidly. A wonderful feeling welled up from between his legs. She was struggling and squirming— and Royce pulled out and came all over her skirt, blouse, his shirt and he didn't know where else.

"You asshole! I told you only just the tip," she screamed, slapping at him.

Royce rolled away—feeling thrilled.

"You got some on my angora sweater!"

That was the first and only time for Royce, but not for wont of trying. He had tidied up the story for Toby and the guys.

"There's the inlet," Toby called out, pointing to some crooked channel markers sticking up on either side of the river. "This way," he called back to Will and Frank. They waved paddles to acknowledge and followed them in.

There wasn't much else but trees and bushes, all the way down to the riverbank. A brown sign denoted it as a nature conservation area; another sign warned no wake, no fishing, no hunting—and from the absence of houses, no people.

They alarmed all varieties of birds, from finches, orioles to red cardinals, and passed cows and horses who regarding them warily atop the muddy banks.

"We're in Wisconsin now," Toby said.

"Oh yeah?" Will called out. "Prove it. Where's the cheese?"

The width of the river varied in many spots. It was as narrow as twenty yards across, with close trees and gnarled roots, and then spread to as wide as 100 yards with farmland as far as the distant upslope of the valley. They paddled through shaded areas, then broke out into open sun bleached stretches. Parts of the river were shallow, perhaps no deeper than three to four feet, with mud bars at the shore. They had to stay in the middle of the river, even though the canoes didn't draw that much water.

"God," Frank said, as an observation. "There's nothing out here."

"It's great," Toby said.

"We're gonna die out here," Will half joked. "And no one will ever find us."

"There's got to be a town up ahead," Frank added.

"I'm hungry," Will said.

After awhile the river became wider and first they passed a shack, then a mobile home, then on the other side a white painted, clapboard cottage. It was a small Wisconsin farm town, which they didn't know the name.

"Hey," Royce pointed. "There's a dam ahead." They could hear the water roaring over the dam.

"Dammit...Dammit," Will couldn't resist saying.

It was a spillway dam, similar to the one in Algonquin. They put in at an open area and got out of the canoes.

"What time do you think it is?" Frank wondered aloud.

"Pretty close to noon," Toby guessed.

"There's a store in that gas station over there," Royce said. We got any money left?"

Hands went into pockets and some bills were held out. It added up to about five dollars.

"Is that all the money we got?" Royce asked, sounding worried.

Will looked at Frank. Frank turned away. "You're holding out, aren't ya, ya farmer?"

"I'm not. I just want to save it for the trip back."

"How much?" Toby asked.

"About...ten bucks," Frank admitted.

"Ten bucks! Why didn't you say something last night." Will raised his fist as if to punch Frank. "I was still hungry and would've liked another cheeseburger." He lowered his fist and shook his head.

"He's right," Royce said. "We're going to need it on the trip back. But geez, Frank, We're all in this together."

"Here," Toby held out his hand. "Give me the money and I'll go to that gas station and get us some food."

Toby trotted off to the station while Royce, Will and Frank pulled the canoes out of the water, around the dam, and up a grassy knoll. They collapsed to the grass and leaned against the canoes. They watched Toby walk back with a paper sack.

"It's picnic time, kiddies," he said, pulling out a loaf of white bread, a package of bologna, cup cakes and two quart bottles of Coke. "I didn't have enough for four bottles, so we can share."

"No crumbs in the Coke," Will said accusingly to Frank.

This was a small, rundown river town, whitewashed and bathed in a shimmering bright and simmering summer sun. All the buildings seemed old, and from a long time ago. The edge of town was visible from the grassy knoll and after the line of gas station, tavern, post office, bank all there seemed to be were endless cornfields; cornfields for miles with concrete silos far away on the horizon. An old rusted red pickup clattered down the street and rolled through the only stop sign, leaving an oily blue cloud as it accelerated.

They ate sandwiches in silence. And once done, Will wanted more. "Man, I was hungry. And still am."

"So?" Frank started cautiously. "We're really going to keep going?"

"Yeah...really, ya 'mo," Toby said, irritated. "The man in the store said we can get to Burlington in a few hours."

"Did you ask how far away Green Bay was from here?" Royce asked, peering into the paper sack and fishing out a cupcake.

"Yeah, I did," Toby said, sharply, snapping off a bite of sandwich. "And he gave me a funny look and didn't say anything."

They finished eating and Royce wrapped up the leftover bread, Will went over to the gas station to use the toilet, Toby and Frank got the canoes put in above the dam. Royce brushed crumbs off his shirt and noticed Frank talking adamantly to Toby. Royce knew he was getting more and more anxious and wanted to turn around and go home. Toby had his hands on his hips and was just shaking his head slowly side to side. It was no use. Frank was crestfallen, but let go of the argument. Royce leaned back and laid his head on his forearm, closed his eyes and let the sun warm his face.

A little while later Toby called out. "Hey, bathing beauty? You ready to roll?"

Royce struggled up. Will was ambling back to the canoes. It was time to get going.

Right away the houses of the small town ended as they paddled upstream. Again, it was farm and pasture with cows, corn, squat green bushy rows of soy beans, rough untended acres, trees and wild vegetation right down to the banks. The river narrowed and in some spots was so overgrown that they paddled through a dark canopy of tree limbs, reeds and green algae and cool air. There were stretches of the river that couldn't draft anything deeper than a canoe. The river seemed still, though they were going up river. Even then they would occasionally hit bottom with their paddles. Through the afternoon they twisted and turned with the river, in and out of shade and sun, without seeing another living soul.

The quiet was getting to Frank.

"Royce?" he called out. "Why don't you serenade us from those drum lessons you've been taking?"

"Yeah," Will chimed in. "C'mon Ringo."

Royce chuckled, stowed his paddle between his knees, and said "okay." He thought back over his lessons and used the sides of the canoe to drum on. First he did a double stroke open roll, starting out slowly, then speeding up. The sound reverberated off the hull of the canoe, bounced off the river and scared up a flight of black crows in a passing cornfield.

Will laughed. "What did those lessons cost you? You ought to get your money back. I can do that."

"Here's another one," Royce said, remembering the pattern of a flam paradiddle, and tapping it out on the canoe.

"That's better..." Will said.

And then Royce tapped out a drag that got Frank clapping when he stopped.

"Are you going to be a big time rock'n roller, Royce?" Toby asked.

"Aw, I don't know. The music just excites me and I want to play. I listen to WLS and the Top 40. But even before that, I listened at night to Ernie Simon's Golden Galaxy of Hits on WJJD. He would play Bo Diddley and Chuck Berry and sometimes even some Muddy Waters."

"Now playing," Toby said in a poor imitation of a radio disc jockey while holding his paddle like a microphone, "at the Tiki Club in downtown Carpentersville...Royce Partridge and the Partridge-tones." Both he and Royce laughed. "At least you have some idea of what you want to do. All I hear, like I told ya, from my dad is get good grades, go to a good college, and get a good job blah blah blah. That's not what I really want to do."

"I bet I know what you really want to do," Royce said, gently paddling a J-stroke to keep the canoe straight.

"Yeah," Toby smiled. "I want to join the army. Ever since I was a little guy I would play army. Loved it. I could even do the manual of arms when I was eight. I get funny looks, but I want to go to Vietnam. I hope there's still a war when I'm old enough to enlist. I want them to escalator.

"You mean, escalate. Not me," Royce shook his head. "No way. I have been taking orders all my life."

"I'll be giving the orders," Toby added.

Behind Will and Frank were mocking Royce, beating on the sides of their canoe and screaming "*She loves you, yeah yeah yeah...*"

"Shut up, you guys," Toby yelled. "I'm getting a headache."

Toward late afternoon they started to see roads along the banks, and an occasional mobile home cut out of the grove of trees.

They pulled into a beach in front of a small weather-beaten cabin, and tied up to the crooked piling of a rundown pier. Royce and Toby walked through knee-high weeds to the cabin and peered in the windows. It was a one-room cabin and vacant. There were papers and layers of dirt all over the linoleum floor.

"I think that duck blind we stayed in was in better shape than this dump," Toby said, his hand to his forehead shielding his eyes against the glass.

"Any food?" Will yelled from the beach.

"Mice, maybe," Royce called back.

"I'm hungry enough to eat a mice."

Frank burst out laughing and Will gave him a look.

Royce walked around to the back of the cabin and saw the back door was ajar. He pushed it as far as it would go and stepped inside. It was dark and smelled of wet and mold. There was a tin sink and short counter to one side. In a far corner sat a low toilet attached by a long pipe and wooden box on the wall above. Spider webs hung from a rusted chain. Flies buzzed at Royce's face. He leaned back and waved them away. Doors and cabinets were open and a chair next to the front door was overturned. The place had been ransacked a long time ago.

A torn newspaper on the counter was dated August 3, 1961. The headline read KENNE and then a long tear, ending with WALL.

Out back two dirt ruts led up a hill and disappeared into the woods.

"Anything in there?" Toby asked as Royce came around to the front.

"Nothing we can use," Royce replied, heading back to the beach.

Will was standing in the river up to his waist. He plunged his hand down to the bottom and scooped up a handful of dripping black mud. He flung it at Frank, who turned quick, avoiding the flying wad.

"Hey!" Frank yelled, wading out into the river and grabbing a pile of mud himself. He heaved it at Will. Will leaned away and the mud splashed behind him. Royce jumped into the water and soon the three were ducking underwater, popping up, giggling like little kids and throwing big globs of mud at each other.

Royce crouched underwater as Will cocked his arm to throw. Royce felt something by his ear. There was a pinch and the sensation of something crawling up his ear. He jumped up and tried to flick whatever it was in his ear out. A wad of mud hit Royce in the shoulder.

"Knock it off! Knock it off!" He yelled.

"What?" Will laughed. "What's the matter?"

"There's something's in my ear," Royce said.

"Mud?" Frank asked.

"No!" Royce was still trying to flick it out with his finger. "I don't know, a fish or something. It hurts."

"A fish?" That made Will laugh harder.

"What's going on?" Toby asked.

"Royce has something in his ear," Frank said, with some concern.

"Lemme see."

Royce was doubled over holding his ear. Every time he moved whatever was in his ear also moved, causing a sharp pain to go down the side of his face and neck.

Toby had Royce's head in both hands and angled it toward the sunlight.

"Awwwww, easy," Royce said.

"I don't see anything," he squinted close. "Wait...there's like a thick black thread in there."

"We got to get him to a hospital." Frank said.

"Where are we going to find a hospital out here?" Will added.

"I know...I know...there's a town ahead," Royce said through clenched teeth.

"Get in the canoes," Toby ordered. "Let's get him to town."

They untied the canoes and clamored in. Royce gingerly stepped into the canoe, holding his head so the thing in his ear didn't move.

"Just steer," Toby said. "I'll paddle."

"Okay." Royce held the paddle alongside the side of the canoe keeping it straight, while keeping his head down and trying to manage the pain.

It wasn't long before they reached town and beached the canoes.

"Frank," Toby said. "You stay with the canoes."

"Okay."

"Yeah," Will added. "Pretend like we're being chased by a gang of hoods."

"Funny," Frank said as the three went up a side street to town.

"Awwwwww, man," Royce groaned, his hand on his ear. "This thing is digging in my head."

They looked up the street and saw a gas station, bar, store, tavern and feed store; then looked down the street. There was a building with a red cross on a white sign marked Clinic.

"Look," Will pointed. He and Toby took Royce under his arms and helped him down the sidewalk to the building. They passed people who stopped and looked after the trio.

Will burst through the clinic door, startling the young girl behind a counter. "Where's the doctor?" he shouted.

Toby led Royce in. Royce looked around and saw an old lady in the waiting room fearfully clutching a small dog in her lap.

"How...how can I help you?" the girl said, standing, looking frightened.

"We need to see a doctor," Will demanded, "Right now!"

"But..." she protested.

"No," he shot back. "My friend needs a doctor...now."

"What's going on in here?" a tall man in white lab coat asked calmly, walking into the waiting room.

"Doctor..." the girl started to say, but Will wheeled on him.

"My friend needs a doctor right now," he said. "Are you the doctor?"

"I am, but," he replied tilting his head forward and looking over his glasses at Will.

"No buts," Will interrupted, standing up to the taller man and giving him a menacing look.

The doctor silently looked down on Will, nonplused he quietly said, "Okay, come into the examining room." Holding open the door he added, "Tell me what happened."

"We were in the river and I felt something crawl into my ear," Royce said.

The doctor motioned Royce to a table in the middle of the room. The receptionist followed them in, but kept her distance from Will.

"Let me take a look see," the doctor slowly said, shining a pen light into Royce's ear.

Royce grimaced and looked around the examining room. It was sparse except for framed pictures of dogs and cats on the walls.

Will and the receptionist exchanged looks. Will's angry face made the girl look away.

"See anything, Doc?" Toby asked.

"Not sure," he slowly said. The doctor turned and whispered something to the receptionist. She went to the counter and cabinet.

"Lay down, son," the doctor said, patting Royce's shoulder.

He was tense and when he moved the thing in his ear moved.

"Awwwwww," he hissed, grimacing.

The receptionist handed the doctor a kidney-shaped stainless steel bowl and large hypodermic needle.

"What're you going to do with that?" Royce said, half rising.

"Easy, son." The doctor settled him back down. "Don't worry, there's no needle."

Suddenly Royce felt something like cold steel being jammed into his ear. He jumped on the table.

"Oh my god," the receptionist squealed, looking into the stainless steel pan under Royce's ear.

"My...my...my," the doctor quietly murmured.

Toby and Will crowded around.

The doctor had filled the hypo with alcohol and squirted it into Royce's ear. A gruesome looking two-inch long insect of some unknown type slid out Royce's ear and now lay dead into a pool of alcohol. It had brown and black feathers on either side of its narrow body and four legs in front and four legs in back, with a tiny green head and antenna.

"What was it? What?" Royce had recovered from the shock of the alcohol. He felt so much better with the bug out of his ear. He rose up and looked into the pan. "That was in my ear?" he said.

The receptionist darted out of the examining room.

"I've never seen anything quite like it," the doctor said.

"Man, that is one ugly bug," Toby said.

"I thought you were faking," Will added.

"Any other bugs in any other orifices, son?" the doctor asked with a grin.

"Naw," Royce chuckled. "Thanks, Doc."

In the distance the sound of a siren could be heard. The three exchanged looks.

"Where'd that girl go?" Will asked.

"Did she call the cops?" Toby said.

The doctor took a step back and placed the pan on the counter.

"We got to get out of here," Toby said, grabbing Royce's arm.

Royce leaped off the table, glancing at the doctor. He leaned against the wall, his arms folded across his chest, a half smile on his lips.

"Thanks again, Doc," Royce said, scrambling after Will and Toby.

The doctor nodded.

The siren was getting louder.

"C'mon," Toby was behind Will at the door.

The little dog on the old lady's lap started yapping.

The doctor followed them into the waiting room and said something to the receptionist behind the counter. They exchanged smiles.

Royce followed Will and Toby out the door, nearly bowling over a woman holding a cat wrapped in a towel.

The siren was getting closer.

The three rounded the corner. Royce stopped a moment, then started to laugh.

"C'mon," Toby called out.

"It's not funny," Will yelled back. "Cops are coming."

Indeed, the siren was getting very loud and Royce glanced around the corner, seeing a red vehicle a block down. Still laughing he made it to the river.

Frank was standing holding the canoes. "What's going on? C'mon. C'mon. We got to get out of here," he was saying.

The siren was on them, screaming and then racing past. As it went by they saw a red pickup truck with Rural Fire Dept. stenciled in white letters on the passenger door.

"Were you guys trying to kill me?" Royce said in mock anger as they paddled out to the middle of the river.

"What?" Will said. "What're you talking about?"

Toby turned and screwed up his face.

"That doctor," Royce explained, chuckling. "Did you see the lady with the dog in the waiting room?"

"Yeah," Will replied.

"And the pictures in the examining room?" Royce went on.

It dawned on Toby and he leaned his head back and laughed aloud.

"Yeah? So what?" Will still hadn't a clue.

"That lady outside? The one with the cat wrapped in a towel?" Royce said. "That doc was a Vet."

"Huh?" Will said.

Frank started to laugh. "You took him to a Vet?"

"Well," Toby struggled to say while laughing. "That was one ugly bug."

"Is that what was in his ear," Frank asked. "A bug?"

"Yeah," Royce said. "One ugly bug and the horse Doc saved me."

"I hope it had babies," Will said, put out.

Royce slapped his paddle in the water and playfully splashed Will.

"We must be getting close to the middle of town, I bet," Toby said.

The river grew wider and soon they were paddling past house after house. Kids were splashing and a dog playfully barked on the riverbank. There was a pair of young boys on a small sailboat, and a powerboat with a water skier. The water skier was a teenage girl in a blue two-piece bathing suit. Her wet blonde hair streamed behind her as she took a wide turn in front of Toby and Royce.

"Hey, babe," Will yelled after her.

She saw Will, smiled and waved.

"Come back!"

Ahead was a town park with a sign saying BURLINGTON, Wis. There was a long asphalt boat ramp, docks, boat club, parking lot, and what looked like a tavern.

Toby suggested they pull in and think about spending the night. They had been paddling for two days and were beginning to feel it. They brought the canoes up onto a grassy area, turned them over and looked around at the bustling town.

"I've never been this far up river...never," Toby quietly said.

"I have never been past McHenry," Frank added. "I think my mom and dad are...."

"Cut it," Will interrupted, throwing a towel at Frank.

"Just saying...they're probably getting worried."

"Not mine," Royce scoffed. "They could give a rat's ass about me. They probably don't even know I'm gone. Soon as I'm done with high school I am outta there."

The sounds of a bat and ball, chatter and a baseball game coming from an old ball field nearby distracted Royce. It was a rundown but classic kelly green and wood ball field, that looked like it needed a couple of coats of paint, some boards on the backstop, infield dirt and grass, new chain link around the outfield and some sweat, affection and care overall. The ongoing game drew him.

"Hey? Where you going?" Toby asked.

"I want to see the game," Royce replied walking away.

He came up to the backstop and saw it was five older black men playing workup. A couple of the men had close cropped gray hair and were dressed in grimy work clothes. There were two players in the outfield, one at second, one pitching and the other batting. All had a rumpled brown paper bag with a beer careful set beside them. A constant chatter was coming from all five positions.

"You can't hit what you can't see," taunted the pitcher.

"Long as you keep holding the damn ball I can't see or hit nothing," the batter replied.

The pitcher stepped back with his hands over his head, then swayed and reached behind, lifted his front knee and stepped toward the plate and threw a slow arcing pitch that made the batter laugh with a toothy smile, then swing....and miss.

"C'mon, man," he complained. "Gimme somethin' straight I can hit."

There was an older darker-skinned man sitting in the stands, smoking a skinny cigarette and sipping from a can of Hamm's. He jumped in to needle the batter.

"I bet this here white boy could hit that," he said. The batter turned with an angry expression.

"Sha-up, Thomas."

"Go on, let the white boy hit."

"No," Royce said, holding his hands up. "Your game. I'm just watching."

"See," The batter picked up the ball and hurled it back to the pitcher. "Even no white boy wants to hit 'gainst your shit. Now," and he tapped the plate with a wood bat. "See if you can get somethin' over the plate."

Royce sat down in the stands. "You guys come here to play all the time?" he asked.

"Mos' every night," Thomas said, taking a pull at his beer, then breathing out smoke from his cigarette "We clocks out at the mill and comes out and let it all hang out. Why you want to know?"

"Just curious—you guys aren't dressed for playing ball."

"Hey, send that white boy out to shortstop," the pitcher called out.

"Thanks, but no glove," Royce replied.

"No glove? Hell," Thomas said. "When we was kids we didn' have no gloves. We used papa's snow gloves, cardboard milk carton or no glove at all. We was fine. Go on out there."

"You sure?" Royce yelled to the pitcher.

"Sure, C'mon," he said with a wave. "You can't be half as bad as them turkeys out there."

That got the two in the outfield indignant. "Turkeys? Who you callin' a turkey. Just throw the damn ball." One of the guys in the outfield had on a beige silk handkerchief tied in the front with tiny knots.

Royce hesitated and looked back to Thomas in the stands. He gave him a nod and in a kind voice said, "You be alrigh'. We just havin' fun."

Royce jogged out to the infield. It was a scrabble; bumpy, weedy field and he took a position at shortstop.

"Hey, he ain' got no socks on," the second baseman said and pointed to Royce. "What happened to yo socks, boy?"

The pace of the game changed. The pitcher's windup was a little more deliberate—and the batter dug in with more determination to hit the ball. The pitch was straight and the batter made contact with a crack, sending a one-hopper up the middle. Instinctively, Royce crossed over and went for the ball. So did the second baseman. He reached out with his left hand, but the ball was by Royce and the second baseman and bouncing out to center. One of the outfielders cut the ball off and fielded it. Royce saw he was using an old, faded, flattened leather three-fingered glove. He tossed it easy to Royce, who caught it and pretended it didn't sting his palm as he turned and threw the ball back to the pitcher.

"He hit that good," Royce said to the second baseman as they walked back to their positions.

"Don' you be tellin' him that," he replied, with a smile. "We'll hear no end of it."

"You gotta be getting' those, white boy," the center fielder was saying. Royce looked back and saw he had a twinkle in his eye. Royce knew he was just teasing. "I wanna just be here, peacefully drinking my beer. I don't wanna be running for no easy ground balls you let get by ya."

Feeling comfortable, Royce called out to the pitcher. "Don't pitch him outside, he'll take that up the middle every time."

The pitcher wheeled around, with a look of mock horror, his mouth wide open showing a row of yellow teeth.

"Listen to the white boy, tellin' me how to pitch." He turned back to the plate. "You gonna see nothin' but smoke on this one."

"Bring it. Here come the hammer."

A couple more hits got through to the outfield then Royce got a two hop ground ball that he fielded smoothly with his bare left hand and snapped a throw back to the pitcher. It caught the pitcher off guard, but he deftly got his glove up and caught the ball. Royce had what felt like bees stinging his bare hand, but he didn't really feel it having made a good play.

They batted around and then asked Royce if he wanted to hit.

"Honestly," he said. "I just like playing defense."

"Go on, get'sum cuts," they were all saying. So Royce went to the plate and took up the old wood bat. It was heavy, with a thick handle. He tapped the rubber home plate, with its curled up corners, and set his feet. Royce kept his wrists loose and swung the bat back and forth before bringing it up to his shoulder just as the pitcher went into his windup. Thwack! The ball was like a bullet by Royce and hit the wooden backstop.

He stepped back and picked up the ball and threw it to the pitcher. The pitcher was smiling. Royce sort of bowed his head and stepped in again.

"Now, C'mon, let the white boy hit," the outfielders were yelling.

The next pitch came in low, slow and fat, and Royce turned on it and with a crack, sent a long fly ball to deep left field. Both outfielders eyes got big and they turned and ran after the ball.

"I'm stopping there," Royce said. "Let someone else hit." He got another smile and one finger salute from the pitcher.

Daylight started to fade and Royce ran off the field and sat down in the stands. The sound of a pop-top being pulled made Royce look over and saw a blue can of Hamm's being offered.

"Thanks...no," he said, regaining his breath, and somewhat surprised at the offer.

"You not gonna drink my beer?"

"I'm only 14!" Royce said, and laughed. That made Thomas laugh as well.

"Well, I ain't gonna let it go ta waste," and he took a long drink. "You ain't like the other white kids from 'round here."

"I'm not from around here and why do you say that?" Royce asked.

"Well, for one thin', they'd be telling us to get off their field. And for 'nother thin', they wouldn't be wantin' to play ball with us."

"Why's that?" Royce wondered aloud.

Thomas regarded him skeptically for a long moment, the beer paused halfway to his mouth. "You really don't know? Do ya?"

"Well, I'm not sure," Royce said. "Is it because you're negroes?"

That got a chuckle, with some beer sputtered out Thomas' mouth. "Nigro?" He wiped his mouth with his sleeve. "Okay. Okay. We're black, ya dig? I know what you mean, and I know you didn't mean no disrespect. Yeah, that's it. They don't want nothin' to do with us."

"But baseball is baseball," Royce said. "It doesn't matter anymore."

"Not to some nowadays, but it does to some aroun' here, and it did when I was your age," he said. "So...what the hell you doin' 'round here?"

"Me and my buddies are on a canoe trip up the river."

"From where?" he asked, taking a quick drink.

"Algonquin."

"Al-gun-quin? Ain' never heard of it," Thomas said. "Hey, Jimmy? You ever hear tell of Al-gun-quin?"

The pitcher stopped mid-motion, thoughtful. Then with his thumb pointing over his shoulder said, "Down a ways in Illinois."

"We're going to canoe all the way to Green Bay."

More beer sprayed behind Thomas' belly laugh. "Green Bay?" he said incredulously. "All the ways to Green Bay on this river?

'Yeah. Why's that funny?"

"This here Fox River?"

"Yeah?" Royce was confused. "Why?"

Thomas sighed. "Boy, you ever done seen a map of the Fox River?"

"Well, no..."

"So's you don' know there's two Fox Rivers in Wisconsin," he said.

"There's what?" Royce didn't understanding. "What do you mean two rivers?"

"Okay." Thomas said, holding up his hand and explaining. "There be the Fox River that comes out of Green Bay—but it don' connect with this here Fox River. In fact, and I hates to be the one tellin' you, but this here Fox River only goes up to 'round Waukesha and then turns into some kind of skinny-ass mud puddle, marsh or somethin' like that. It don' go all the ways to no Green Bay...not at all."

Royce was stunned. He sat silent for a minute, staring off. "You sure?" he hesitantly asked.

"Boy—I done worked in pulp mills and tanneries all up and downs this lower Fox River." Thomas drained his beer. "It gets close to Waukesha and ain' nothing but a ditch. Honest to God, kid."

Royce was confused, not knowing what he should do with this information. What would he tell Toby and the others. He stood up and thanked the guys on the field with a wave. They waved back. "Go on get yoursef' a pair of socks, white boy," the second baseman yelled back with a laugh. Royce held out his hand to Thomas in the stands.

"Thanks for letting me play and thanks for telling me about the river."

"Hey, alrigh'." Thomas shook his hand. "Sorry to disappoint you 'bout the river. Take care of yourself now."

"You too."

Royce walked away from the ball field, his thoughts all jumbled up, not knowing what to do with what Thomas had told him. It would just crush Toby if he told him. Toby, Frank and Will were laying around the canoes, in the shade. Will was dozing. Toby was eating some bread left over from lunch, not listening to Frank who was talking quietly to him.

"She lives across the street and I'm thinking of asking her out..." Frank was saying.

Royce, tensely, sat down next to Toby.

"Where you been?" Toby asked.

"I was playing ball with some black guys over there," he replied.

"You mean colored guys?" Toby asked, surprised.

"No, black guys," Royce said. "They want to be called black. They were pretty cool."

Frank laughed. "What were they playing Hit the Honky?"

"No, they were okay guys, just playing workup after working all day." The weight of what Thomas said about the river lay heavy on Royce. Should he say something, he wondered?

"You're lucky you didn't get a knife in the back," Toby said.

"Or raped," Frank chipped in.

"Raped?" Royce exclaimed. "Knifed? What're you guys talking about? One guy offered me a beer. But I didn't take it."

That woke Will up. "A beer! And you didn't take it?"

"I don't want a beer," Royce replied.

Dusk was settling in, the air becoming cool and humid. The sky turned from bright to a deep blue.

"Are we going to spend the night here?" Royce asked Toby.

"May as well," he said, sighing. "I'm beat."

"Yeah, me too," Frank added.

"Didn't take a beer," Will mumbled, slipping back into sleep.

In a few minutes Frank and Toby had joined Will in sleep. But Royce, though tired, couldn't sleep. He wrestled with what he'd been told about the Fox River not going all the way to Green Bay. Should he wake Toby and tell him? No, he'd wait for morning, he'd know what to do then. Toby would be disappointed, maybe even angry. Worse, he'd feel like a fool for having pushed them on this journey. Perhaps it was better to say nothing and wait until they reached the end of the river. Royce didn't know. Toby may not even believe him. They may have to paddle all the way to the marsh or mud puddle like Thomas said. Maybe in the morning; maybe he'd tell them in the morning. After a long while, looking up to the dark sky and stars, Royce drifted off to sleep.

{-10-}

Royce woke with a start. Someone was tugging on his arm.

"Get under the canoe," Toby whispered. "There's a cop car driving by."

Royce scrambled under the overturned canoe.

"Will?" Toby hissed. "Get Frank. Get under the canoe."

A searchlight beam flicked over the boat ramp and grassy area. Under the canoe, the white light made shadows dart back and forth, up and down. But the circle of light didn't stop on the canoes. They heard the crunch of gravel as the patrol car slowly made a turn around the parking lot. Red light from the rear of the patrol car cast an eerie glow inside the canoe. Then, it was dark.

"I told ya. I told ya we should've headed back." Frank said to Will.

They rolled out from under the canoes. Toby stretched.

"Frank wants to go home," Will said.

"Frank wanted to go home yesterday. We're not going home," Toby replied with a yawn. "We're too close to turn back."

"Well—that woke me up," Royce said, shivering in the early morning chill.

"We may as well put the canoes in and paddle up river," Toby suggested.

Royce shrugged, remembering what Thomas had said about the river not going all the way to Green Bay. Should he say something?

Frank looked upset. "Alright, may as well keep going."

They pushed the canoes down the dew-wet grass and into the river and stepped in and glided to the middle of the narrow river. The town lights and house lights left on overnight lit the banks of the river and shimmered off the dark water. Quietly, they paddled, skirting the lights. Royce looked over his shoulder and saw the shadowy outlines of Frank and Will off to his left and a canoe length behind. Silent, except for the plash of the canoe paddles, they eased through town. Houses were scattered at first, then some businesses, then the town center was behind them and fewer and fewer houses, finally a vacant lot and darkness. The moon, a sliver now, low and waning, shone off the river as they steered for it.

"It's really dark," Royce said. "Can you see?" He asked Toby.

"Enough," he responded.

"We don't have any running lights. Hope we don't meet any other boats."

"We won't. It's too shallow for powerboats."

The moon set and the night was black. Using the dark tree shadows on either bank against the lighter horizon, they stayed to the middle of the river. Every so often a street light from a roadway intersection would give them light and direction. But mostly, they were blind. Their silence was broken by something jumping and splashing back into the water.

"What was that?" Frank froze.

"A duck farted," Will said. "Now, shut up."

Royce gave a quiet laugh. "Probably a fish. Relax."

After awhile the dark turned to an inky blue. Toby, a dark shadow at the bow, slowly became visible. Glancing back, Royce could make out Frank in the bow of the canoe. A white fog was rising from the river. They paddled through it, parting the fog in swirls. The morning cool made the canoe bead up and water droplets run down the silver sides.

"What's that book," Royce asked. "Where some guy goes up an African river?"

"No school stuff," Will protested.

"With Humphrey Bogart?" Frank guessed.

"No, that's the African Queen."

"Who's a queen?" Will shot back.

"You are, ya 'mo."

"No, there's a book where this guy goes up river and is never heard from again."

"Great," Toby said. "They took canoes up the Fox River to Green Bay...and were never-heard-from-again."

They all laughed.

Cort Fernald

The river twisted and turned and began to narrow for long stretches. In the center of the river they could reach out and touch tree limbs from either bank.

Royce, thinking, again debated whether to tell Toby they would run out of river soon. But again, he decided against it. He rationalized that Toby wouldn't believe him.

Ahead, as the morning sun filtered through the leaves, they saw a fork in the river. The widest branch of the fork looked shallow, with rocks and a mud bar. There was a channel to one side, near the bank. The left fork was narrow, but appeared deeper. Toby put his paddle across the hull and stood up. They drifted to the middle of the fork. He was quiet, looking to the right branch, and then the left.

"What do we do?" Frank asked.

"When you see a fork in the river...?" Will said.

"Take one," Royce answered. "But...which?" He was thinking this might be where the lower Fox River started its end. They waited for Toby; even though it was obvious they had to go to the left. Trees followed the river to the right, while the left fork went off into open farmlands.

"Left," Toby said decisively, sitting and taking up his paddle. He dug into the water on the right side of the canoe, swinging the bow toward the deeper fork.

They broke out of the trees and shade into sunshine and cornfields going up the valley. The river couldn't have been more than 20 yards bank to bank, but a channel ran deep and true. They made good progress. Occasionally, they would pass galvanized irrigation pipes laid from the fields and into the river. A murder of crows scattered out of the

{ 156 }

corn stalks and took to the sky. Sunlight gave their black wings an iridescent sheen.

Then the channel became narrower and narrower, with high banks and tall weeds growing along the shoreline. Up ahead they saw a concrete embankment with a rusted lock and wheel. It was a dead end to the river.

"We've got to turn around," Toby suddenly said; then yelled back to Will and Frank. "Turn around. Go back to the fork. This is the wrong way."

With some difficulty, because of the narrowness of the channel, Will and Frank managed to turn their canoe around.

"Hey, Toby," Royce called. "Just turn in your seat. I'll take the bow."

Royce was now in front and paddled right after Will and Frank.

"How'd you get in front?" Will asked Royce. "Did you guys change seats?"

"Did you hear that?" Royce chuckled, asking over his shoulder to Toby.

"Yeah," Toby replied. But he wasn't laughing.

They paddled back to the fork and drifted out to the middle. Without saying anything, Royce and Toby turned in their seats, with Toby again taking the bow.

"We may have to carry the canoes over that sand bar," he said. There was a deep trough along the steep bank. Tree roots and large rocks were exposed along the bank. They paddled up to the shallows and the bow crunched into sand. Toby got out and Royce climbed over the seat in the front and stepped onto the sand bar. They wrestled the canoe by its cross bars, slipping on the river rocks.

"This sucks," Royce said breathing heavily.

"No shit, Sherlock," Toby agreed.

They reached the far end of the sand bar and found a wide area, which appeared deep enough for the canoes. They put in and paddled upriver and around a bend. Then came another stretch of shallows, and they had to muscle the canoes over rocky shoals. No one spoke, and all that could be heard was huffing from exertion. The sand became black mud, soft and sucking mud. Upfront Toby was struggling, sinking to his shins in the black river mud. There was a clearing up river, with no trees to block their view and they saw as far as the river ran rocks and mud and the trickle of a current--no channel and no deep water.

Toby stopped, dropping the bow of the canoe. His shoulders sagged and his head went down. His whole body seemed to slump.

"I can't believe it," he said over and over, staring at the black muck.

Royce glanced back and traded concerned looks with Will and Frank. They stood there in ankle deep mud, breathless and silent, looking at Toby.

"Toby?" Royce called after awhile. "Toby?"

Slowly, Toby looked up.

"It's as far as we can go," He said. "The river ends."

"But..." Toby said, disbelieving. "I saw on a map...the Fox River coming from Green Bay."

"You sure they were connected? C'mon..." Royce said to Will and Frank. "We've got to go back to the fork...and then head back to Algonquin."

"Aw!" Frank started to exclaim, but was cut short as Will and Royce turned on him. "...right." He ended softly.

Toby stood facing the shallow river, shaking his head.

"Toby?" Royce struggled through the mud to him. "It's been a blast...but we gotta go back now." He reached out and tried to turn Toby around.

"I don't understand," he said. "I can show you on a map."

"I believe you," Royce replied. "Maybe the river's just low this time of year...or something."

Toby turned and picked up the bow of the canoe and slogged back over the mud bar, slipping on the rocks, sand and mud.

"I'll take the bow for awhile," Royce said, carrying the stern of the canoe.

"Yeah," Toby answered quietly. "That's okay."

At the fork Royce brought the stern of the canoe around and put in behind Will and Frank's canoe and stepped to the bow. Their legs were covered in black mud. They washed off. Then Toby clambered into the back. They were paddling with the current, and knowing the river they made good time—reaching Burlington and going through Wilmot within hours. They had plenty of daylight left. Will and Frank were happily chattering, while Royce and Toby paddled in silence. Occasionally, Royce called back to Toby "you alright?" He would get a grunt, or a "yeah", but it was apparent Toby was still disappointed.

Royce, though he wouldn't admit it, was relieved he didn't have to tell Toby that he knew eventually the river would end.

"I'm okay," Toby said. "I swear. I saw on a map that the Fox River went to Green Bay."

"No prob," Royce replied, fighting the urge to tell him there were really two Fox rivers. "The river must be low. It's been a blast. But next year..." Royce paused.

"Yeah?" Toby asked.

"Next year, when we get our learner's permit...let's take a car..."

That made Toby snort, a little laugh. Will and Frank, leading the way, turned and looked back wondering what was so funny.

The current at their backs, and the push of an occasional valley wind, they made only one stop, for Will to get food at the same gas station they stopped at yesterday. It was late afternoon when they reached the Chain O' Lakes.

Toby paddled at the back of the canoe in silence. The mood in Frank and Will's canoe was the complete opposite. They traded jibes and were splashing each other.

Powerboats were racing all over the lakes, with water skiers, or partiers speeding by, waving with drinks or beers in hand. The wakes from all the powerboats rocked the canoes back and forth and side to side.

"Turn to the wake," Royce called out to Will and Frank.

Coming up slowly alongside was a large cabin cruiser. It blasted its horn, and Toby angled the canoe away. Lounging at the steering wheel on the flying bridge of the cabin cruiser, an older man gave Royce and Toby a lazy wave. Royce returned the wave, but he was eyeing the large wake rolling toward them.

All of a sudden Toby was half-standing and waving his arms at the cruiser. The cruiser throttled back and they rode the wake toward the high stern of the cruiser.

"Hey!" Toby called out, "are you going down as far as the McHenry locks?

Royce grabbed onto the side of the cruiser, keeping the canoe from crashing into it. He noticed painted on the back of the boat was My Other Gal from McHenry, Ill.

The driver nodded, shouting back. "I am. What can I do for you? You want a ride?"

"How about a tow?" Toby asked.

The driver considered a moment, then motioned to Will and Frank to paddle closer. "I think that can be arranged," he said, sliding down the ladder from the flying bridge. He took a coil of rope and tossed it out to Royce.

"Thanks" they called out.

"You boys must be tuckered out." He said, tying the other end of the rope onto an aft cleat. "Play that out a long ways or the wake will swamp you."

They looped the rope to Royce and Toby's canoe and Will and Frank tied it to the bow loop on their canoe.

The driver climbed back into the seat on the bridge, settled in and slowly eased the throttle forward. The rope went taut from the water and with a jerk the canoes went forward. All four almost fell over backwards, but held on.

The canoes were far enough back to ride on the high middle wake, nestled in the calm water between a white foam Vee. The driver looked back, raising his hand and gesturing with an OK sign.

Toby waved back OK and glanced back at Will and Frank, who waved they were alright.

"This is great," Royce yelled back, trying to be heard over the cruiser's engine noise, the wind and the canoe loudly cutting through the hard surface of the water.

What had taken them nearly a day and a half paddling against the current upriver, took only two or three hours. They reached McHenry still in daylight. The big cruiser started to slow, then idled as the driver jumped down and motioned for them to untie the rope. They untied and he coiled the wet rope over his forearm, then spun it with the last few feet of rope, finishing in a tight bundle.

"Thanks," the four called out, waving to the driver as they paddled by.

"You betcha," he said, climbing up into the driver's seat and easing the throttle forward, turning toward a marina in McHenry.

The locks were just ahead and they put in to portage. They dragged the canoes around the locks and downhill to the muddy path.

"Crap," Will complained. "This canoe is getting heavier and heavier."

"This is good," Toby said, stepping past Royce and climbing into the front seat of the canoe. Royce stood back with hands on hips, surprised Toby took the bow. "We'll be back in Algonquin around midnight," he added. Royce pushed off and stepped into the rear seat. They glided out into the river, waiting for Will and Frank to put in.

There wasn't a lot of daylight left, as the sun set orange on the horizon. A few powerboats, with green and red running lights, passed them going upriver.

"I wonder what I'm facing when we get back," Frank said.

"You're grounded, young man," Will volunteered, trying to sound like an adult. "Grounded until you're 21!"

They passed under the Cary bridge, then the railroad bridge just as night was closing in. It was misty and cool on the river. They knew they were getting closer.

Coming around Haegar's Bend was not as rough or chancy as when they were going up the river. With the wind at their backs, the current pulled them in and through the swift choppy waters. They were around and out with little trouble.

The lights of Algonquin could be seen in the distance as the river calmed. Crickets, frogs on the banks, the far sounds of cars and the easy splash of their paddles were the only sounds as they came nearer to Recharge Resort.

"Over there," Royce whispered, not really knowing why he was whispering.

"Yeah, I see it." Toby pointed with his paddle. "Hey," he said quietly, turning back to Frank and Will. "Follow us in."

"Gotcha," Frank said in an undertone.

They angled to shore and reached the pebble beach, hitting shore with a crunch.

Toby climbed out and pulled the canoe up the beach to the dark embankment, while Royce jumped out the back end. Frank came in after and stepped onto shore.

"Let's just leave them," his voice was shaky, "and get the hell out of here."

"No—we have to put them back. It'll be the perfect crime. No one will know we took them," Toby said.

"C'mon, man," Will whined. "Let's just leave them. They'll find them tomorrow."

Royce took the wet towels, rope and bucket from the canoes and chucked them into the bushes. Toby's silence meant no to Will and Frank, and he wasn't changing his mind. Royce tore the duct tape covering Recharge Resort off each canoe and threw the wad of tape in the river.

A single white light bulb burned brightly at the gate to the resort. The caretaker's house, up the slope and in the woods, was dark, except for a faint light in a second floor window.

With Royce at the front, Toby at the back, they lifted the canoe and scrambled up the embankment and across River Road. They were just out of the circle of white light, in shadows by the chain link fence.

"Frank," Toby whispered. "Get over the fence and..."

"Why me?" Frank protested. "Why is it always me?"

"Shut up, ya 'femme," Will added, giving him a shove. "Just do it."

"Okay okay," he said grappling over the fence and jumping down inside the resort grounds. "C'mon...let's do this quick."

Royce and Toby stood the canoe on end and carefully rested it against the fence.

"Will?" Royce whispered. "Let's get the other one." They both dashed across the road and down the embankment.

"Hurry up," Frank urged.

"Relax, man," Toby said.

Royce and Will were back in minutes, carrying the second canoe across the road. Setting it aside, Royce realized Frank wouldn't be able to handle the canoe coming over the fence all by himself. "I'm coming over," he said, climbing the chain link and letting himself down.

Toby and Will took the first canoe and tipped it over the fence. "Don't scrape it, this time," Royce said, taking the end and walking it backward hand over hand. Frank reached up for the back end coming off the fence. He got the canoe and almost dropped it.

"Careful," Royce hissed.

They backed up and set the canoe down near the racks. Something came over the fence and hit the dirt near Royce. It was one of the paddles, with three more following.

Toby and Will had the second canoe going up and over the fence.

"Take the back end," Royce whispered to Frank.

The canoe came over and Royce reached up and caught the canoe as it came off the fence. He turned at his end, but Frank was walking backward.

It may have been one step, or maybe two steps backward, but suddenly the canoe flipped out of Royce's grasp. He saw Frank stumbling back, tripping over a rock. It was probably only a few seconds, but it seemed like slow motion and long minutes as the canoe fell and landed with a loud, hollow, resounding ka-boom on the other canoe. It seemed to echo all over the valley. He was instantly brought back to his senses hearing the caretaker's dog barking wildly, and lights going on all over the place.

"Shit!" Royce yelled. He could see Frank sprawled on his back. "Get up! Get up!" Royce reached out for Frank.

"Get the hell out of there, you guys," Toby shouted outside the fence.

Frank got to his feet and was right next to Royce at the fence. They both went over quickly, almost pulling the fence down as they did. Will and Toby could be seen down River Road on a dead run. The dog was loose, barking and running after them. Frank sprinted past Royce and down the road. Royce's heart was pounding and he was running as fast as he could.

Headlights flashed down River Road, approaching fast, with red lights spinning. No one needed to say it, but someone called out "Cops!"

Royce leapt off the road, into bushes and trees on the embankment. It was rough and steep and he slid, grabbing hold of a sapling. Not one cop car, but two, roared past. The second cop car braked to a screeching halt no more than ten yards from Royce's hiding place.

A car door slammed. Royce heard the cop walking on the road.

He lay in the brush, under cover of darkness, holding his breath, not making a sound. Royce held tightly to the sapling or he would've slid down the bank and into the river. The cop was getting near. Something was stinging Royce's bare arm. Yellow light from a flashlight was shining in and out of the bushes. In a quick pass of the light Royce saw ants, red ants, all over his arm. They were biting, but he dare not move. He bit his lower lip. The cop walked past on the road above and slowly went back down the road.

It was quiet, except for crickets and the caretaker's dog barking in the distance. A car door slammed. Royce took the opportunity to rise up and brush the ants off his arm. He waited. The car ignition started up. After a few minutes he worked his way up the bank. Crouching behind a tree he looked down River Road and saw the cop car easing down the road toward town. The car went round a bend. Should he wait? It was dark again. Should he make a break for it? What happened to the others? He thought if he saw the cop car again he could jump into cover. So he broke from behind the tree and hit the road running.

He was running hard and went round the bend in the road—and was blinded by a searchlight and a shout of "Stop...or I will shoot!"

Royce staggered to a stop and put his hand up to shield his eyes from the light. He could barely make out the silhouette of a pudgy Algonquin police officer, one hand on the butt of his holstered revolver, the other hand working the searchlight on the side of the cop car.

"Shit," Royce breathlessly said, hands on his knees, catching his breath.

"Shit is right, son," the cop said. "And you're in it up to your eyebrows. Get your hands up and walk toward me."

Royce went forward with his hands up, to the car.

"Turn around. Put your hands behind your back."

Royce complied and had handcuffs clamped tightly on his wrists. "I wasn't doing anything."

"Yeah, I know—shut up and get in the car." The cop opened the back door and gave Royce a shove in.

He sprawled across the backseat, landing against Will. Will was also cuffed. Royce struggled up. He looked and saw Toby in the front seat. Toby had his elbow on the armrest, his head in his hand. Royce noticed Toby wasn't cuffed.

"What happened?" Royce asked him.

"We got caught."

Royce looked over at Will. He was looking away, out the window, saying nothing.

The cop grunted as he plopped into the driver's seat. "Two down, one more to go," he said. "Right?" He asked, glancing over at Toby.

He started the car and keeping the headlights off, eased down River Road. Soon, in a streetlight ahead, a lone figure was seen running. It was Frank. "That the last one?" he said over to Toby. Toby nodded. The cop put the car in neutral and noiselessly eased down the road. When he was close enough, he snapped on the headlights and searchlight. Frank looked back, his eyes large with fear. He stumbled and stopped.

"Hold it right there, kid," the cop called over a loudspeaker. He stopped the car, left it running and set the parking brake. Royce watched through the windshield as the cop spun Frank around and cuffed him. He led him to the back door, opened it and pushed him in.

"I wasn't..." Frank said.

"Shut it," the cop said, slamming the back door and groaning as he dropped into the driver's seat. He unhooked a handset and clicked on his radio. "Car four. Car four," he said. "I've got Baby Face Nelson and his gang..." he smirked at his own joke. "And I am headed back to the station."

"Car four over," was the reply crackling over the radio.

"We weren't doing anything," Royce said.

"I told you to shut up," the cop said, putting the car in gear and accelerating. "Tell it to your parents when we get back to the station."

They passed the road to Toby's house, then Wood Street where Royce's house was. Someone was sniffling, crying. Royce looked over and in the light of a passing streetlight saw tears glistening down Will and Frank's cheeks.

There was hardly any traffic on the road. They pulled off River Road and went over the bridge into town. The cop pulled the car to the front of the police station. It was late, after two in the morning; the lights of Elektra's restaurant across the street were dark and the parking lot empty. The cop got out and pulled Frank, Royce and Will from the back seat one after the other. Toby opened the passenger door and stood on the other side of the cop car.

"Alright, inside," the cop said.

Looking back, Will asked, "how come he isn't wearing..."

"Shut up!" the cop said, punctuating it with a kick to Will's butt propelling him through the door and into Frank and Royce inside the police station. The door behind slammed.

The squad room was bright and hot. A chest-high counter cut the room in half. There were desks littered with papers and file folders behind the counter. In the corner a bank of radio equipment snapped with static. The brown and white checkered linoleum tile was dirty and stained in spots. The air was close with thin wisps of cigarette smoke drifting over the desks. It smelled of burnt coffee. The walls were cluttered with a girly calendar, notes, shift schedules and a disarray of black and white wanted posters.

An older, balding cop with a red face and beady eyes, stood up from a desk.

"Well, well, well, the Dillinger gang," he said, more in weariness than mockery.

The other cop lifted an apron on the high counter and grabbed a ring of keys from a hook behind the counter.

Will, Royce and Frank, still in handcuffs, stood with slumped shoulders and looking down to the floor, in the center of the squad room. Toby stood casually, near them but away from them. Frank, sniffing, was still teary. Royce turned his head sideways and looked at Toby. He wouldn't look at him. Royce glanced at Will, and he shrugged.

"Alright, on the bench," the older cop said, pointing to a worn wooden bench. The other cop came around with the keys and unlocked the handcuffs.

"You first, son" the older cop said, motioning Toby to the counter. "Give me your name, address and phone number."

Each was separately called to the counter.

"What's your name?" he asked Royce.

"Royce Partridge," he answered, rubbing his wrists where the cuffs had cut him. "3 Wood Street. My phone number? Good luck getting a hold of my parents."

The cop stopped writing and looked at Royce without raising his head. "Why? Not home?"

"You'll find out," Royce said, reciting his phone number.

The older cop's head came up quick and tilted to one side. He regarded Royce with narrow eyes and pursed lips. "Sit down, wise guy," he said finally. "You, cry baby—come up here."

Banging in through the door came another cop, shorter and with a military crew cut. He paused a moment and looked at Will and Royce on the bench, then went to a water cooler and pulled water into a paper cup.

"We're going to call your parents," the older cop told them. "We're going to figure out what kind of crime wave you juvenile delinquents have been on. Meanwhile, you'll be held here."

"Where do you want'em, Chief?"

"That one" he pointed to Toby, "sit him in the office. Those two can stay here...and put the wise guy..." he flipped his finger at Royce, "in the cage."

The pudgy cop took Toby into a side office, while the short cop came up to Royce and grasped his upper arm, jerking him up from the bench. He was taken to a small room with no windows, where, in the middle of the room was a six foot by six foot cage made of four inch iron bands. The cage was old, with layers of brown paint and orange rust at the seams and corners. There was only a single wooden stool in the center of the cage.

Royce balked. "I gotta go to the bathroom," he said.

The short cop bent to unlock an old padlock on the low cage door. He straightened up. "Yeah, alright. That door over there. I'll be outside."

Royce went into the bathroom and unzipped his cutoffs. It smelled like an outhouse. He was scared, and had difficulty peeing. The toilet was old, with a wooden tank and chain. The bowl was stained brown. There was no window. If there had been a window, and if it was big enough, Royce would've been out it. He finally peed and pulled the chain. Coming out he heard the tall cop behind the counter talking to someone on the phone.

"Yeah, he's here. Come on down and collect him."

The short cop was waiting, leaning against the cage door. He was smoking and crooked his finger for Royce to get into the cage. Royce stooped down and stepped into the cage. The door clanked behind him and the padlock clattered closed. He sat on the stool and let out a long sigh.

Time passed, first with Frank and then Will coming in to use the bathroom. Both whispered to Royce as they went by, "you okay?" Royce answered with a quiet "yeah". Toby came in, went to the bathroom, and left the room without saying anything, not even looking at Royce. He tried to distract himself, thinking about his favorite songs and quietly tapping the snare and cymbal on his knees, his right foot doing 4/4 time, with his left working the high hat. But he couldn't concentrate.

Frank's dad was the first to arrive at the station. He was somber and spoke in soft tones with the tall cop behind the counter. Royce caught snatches of the conversation. No charges for theft were being filed, but they could be charged with trespass and criminal mischief. Frank's dad nodded, then went over to Frank on the bench and stood in front of him. Frank had his head bowed. Will sat next to him, looking away. Words were exchanged in undertones, with Frank nodding and then standing. "Your mother and I have been worried sick." He shuffled out the squad room with his father behind.

It was quiet again, except for the crackle of the radio, the hum of florescent lights and someone hunting and pecking on a typewriter.

There was a commotion and loud voice when Toby's dad came in. "Where is he? Where's that little shit?"

Toby's dad looked around for Toby, but caught sight of Royce in the cage. "Oh, I might've known you were behind this." Toby came up next to his father. He got a slap on the side of the head. "And what did you do now?" Toby stumbled sideways with the slap. His dad got behind him and shoved Toby toward the door.

Passing the open door he glared at Royce. "That cell suits you," he spat out. "I had you pegged as trouble for my boy. Don't ever come round the house again. You got me?"

The condemning words might've stung Royce some other time. Now—it didn't have any affect.

"Bill...Junior...thanks for looking out for my boy. Bring your car to the shop and I'll take care of ya."

"You bet," one cop said.

"Get in the car," Toby's dad said with a push. "Your mother was worried about you."

It was just Will and Royce. Royce sat with his elbows on his knees, his chin in his hands. Will squirmed on the wooden bench.

Blue cigarette smoke drifted past Royce. He glanced up to the door. The short cop was standing in the doorway, smoking.

"We called your house," he said in a low voice. "Took us a couple of calls to get someone to answer."

The station door opened and Will's dad walked in. Right away there was a heated exchange between them.

"Are they always like that?" the short cop asked Royce.

"Who them?" He said motioning toward Will and his dad.

The cop smoked, not saying anything for a while. "No, your parents. Anyway," he finally said. "Once we were able to talk to your dad, he said..." He paused a moment, studying his cigarette. "He said let the little bastard rot in jail and hung up."

Will's dad had him by the collar was manhandling him out the squad room and to the parking lot, all the while lecturing him on using his head, not doing what others do and knowing right from wrong. "What is the matter with you?" he said aloud. "What am I going to tell your mother?"

"We called back and tried to talk to your mother—but she was..." He stopped when Royce angrily looked up at him.

The tall cop came up behind the short cop. "They're just kids, Jimmy. Cripes, you remember all the shit we pulled when we were their age?" They looked at each other and smiled. "Remember the time we put that scare crow out at Cherry Corners and watched from the cornfield as all the cars came round the corner, hit the brakes and went into the ditch? My dad broke his belt on my butt."

"Hey, wise guy?" he said to Royce. His tone was different, more in a joking manner. "You hungry? We got some pop, doughnuts or a bag of chips?"

Royce glanced from short cop to the tall one. They both had expressions of sympathy, friendliness. It made him feel all the more ashamed. "No...no thank you. I'm okay."

The short cop flicked ash off the end of his cigarette and regarded it thoughtfully.

"Suit yourself," the tall cop said, turning away, muttering to himself. "Thanks me, that's the most polite villain I've ever met."

"We've seen your record, kid. How many times have you run away?" The other cop said.

Royce didn't answer.

"Ya know...there are people you can talk to. People that can help," he said, waiting for a response. After a few minutes and no response, he took a drag on his cigarette and went back into the squad room.

Alone, Royce folded his arms on his knees and lay his head down. Softly, his breath shuddering in his lungs, and so no one could hear, he started to cry. No one would see. No one will ever know. Soon, he slept.

The sound of the key in the padlock woke Royce. He rubbed sleep from his eyes. This was a different cop.

"Wake up, son," he said to Royce, opening the cage door. "Your father's here. C'mon out."

Royce was stiff and sore and stooped stepping out of the cage. His father was at the counter. He was in a suit, dressed for work. Last night he was a sloppy drunk, his hair wild, his eyes bloodshot, yelling and swearing, telling the cops on the phone to let Royce rot in jail. But now, as the daylight filtered through the Venetian blinds and hurt Royce's eyes, he was the picture of a model citizen.

"And if there are charges you will inform us what our next step is?" He glanced at Royce crossing the squad room. His eyes were hard. "I am very sorry for the trouble he has caused you," he said to another cop leaning against the counter, cradling a cup of coffee. "We don't seem to be able to...to...handle him. We've sent him to a psychologist and counselors but nothing seems to get through." He sounded apologetic to the cops, but the undertone was that it wasn't his fault.

Standing back and behind his father he noticed the cops were new, from the morning shift. They just listened, not saying anything, expressionless.

His father turned to Royce and his expression instantly changed to anger. Then he was back talking to the cops, saying how sorry he was for Royce's behavior.

"I've got to go to work, can I just take him, then?"

"Sure, Mr. Partridge. We will notify you if charges are filed, and whether it's a fine or some kind of community service."

"Well, thank you, thank you, officers." Royce's father stepped about face and hissed low "c'mon, you." He walked past Royce and out the squad room quickly, with Royce trailing. As he went out the door Royce glanced back and saw the cops standing there, watching.

"You little fuckin' bastard," his father spat out when they were in the parking lot. "You do nothing but shame and embarrass me. I should've told the cops to lock you up and throw away the key," he violently jerked open the car door.

Royce opened the passenger door and slid into the seat.

"Are you going to start this again," his father barked. "You need to straighten up and fly right. This isn't Park Forest and we're not moving again."

"Why are you bringing up Park Forest," Royce shot back. "That wasn't my fault."

"That's not what the cops said," he father snarled.

"The cops!" Royce said. "I didn't throw the match in the gasoline, another guy did. They all ran away. I stayed and tried to put the fire out. I'm the one that stayed."

"I ought to smack you," his father shouted, his right arm raised.

"Do it," Royce dared, glaring at him.

After a long tense moment, his father's arm slowly went down. He turned the key in the ignition, still fuming. "I'm going to be late for work. Who knows how much damage you did this time. What's it going to cost me," he grumbled. "You're a curse. A god damn curse I have to live with." He screeched the wheels backing out of the police station parking lot and jammed the car into first gear.

"Hey!" Someone yelled at Royce. Startled, he looked up to the bank. "This is private property."

"What?" Royce said, turning around at the end of the pier. On the bank was a young boy with short spiky hair, astride a BMX bicycle. "Oh...I know. I'm sorry. I was just taking a break from my run." Royce stood, stiffly.

"You're trespassing," the boy said mustering a tone of authority.

"Hey, relax, kid," Royce replied, walking up the pier. "I'm going." He stepped off the pier and climbed the gravel bank onto River Road.

The boy backed up now that Royce was close.

"I used to live around here," he said, hands on his hips, nodding up toward Wood Street.

"Oh yeah? In Algonquin?" the boy asked skeptically. "When was that?"

"That was...once upon a time," Royce replied, shaking the stiffness from his arms and legs and slowly jogging off.

It was after one, maybe two weeks of being grounded that Royce heard a moped revving up the driveway to his house. It was Toby.

"Hey," Royce said, opening the door, glad to see him.

"Hey," Toby replied, with a wide engaging smile.

"I thought you weren't supposed to hang out with me?"

"I'm not," Toby said. "You're the kid parents won't let their kids play with," he added with a snorting chuckle. "And what the old man doesn't know--never happened. Will and Frank are down at Eddy's Arm Pit, want to go?"

"Sure," Royce replied.

"Hop on," Toby was walking back to his moped.

"Wait a minute," Royce said, disappearing into the house. A few minutes later Royce pushed up the garage door and rolled out a new red moped.

"Well, look at you," Toby laughed. "When'd you get it?"

"A few days ago," Royce said, hopping on and peddling the engine to life."

"Let's go!" Toby shouted over the engine noise.

Off they roared with a loud high-pitched whine in a cloud of blue smoke.

There were no criminal charges filed, but the four were ordered by the court to do two weeks community service. The community service consisted of cleaning up Recharge Resort and preparing it for the off season. The caretaker, wearing thick bifocal lens, his dog on a chain, a shotgun tucked under his arm, stood by like he was guarding a Louisiana chain gang while Royce, Toby, Will and Frank raked leaves, swept out cabins, hosed down and put up the canoes in the boathouse, covered the swimming pool and played with the caretaker's dog as he snoozed under the cool shade of a large oak. After three days there wasn't much left to do. So the caretaker wagged his finger at them menacingly and told them never do it again, then waved the back of his hand and said, "go away, you're done." The dog cried as they left.

The four remained friends throughout high school, but through the years started going their separate ways.

Royce's drumming got him into some bands and small combos and hanging out with musicians. It was a different crowd.

Toby played sports, but never really excelled beyond being very good, though not great. He and Royce occasionally double-dated, only when Royce wasn't playing a party or a high school dance.

True to his word on the morning of his eighteenth birthday Toby went down to join the army. But the army told him they had their quota for the next six months and he should come back. Not to be deterred he joined the National Guard instead. He still wanted to go to Vietnam but that wasn't going to happen in the National Guard. And that was when he rescued Royce from the Canal Street Bridge during the Democratic convention in Chicago. He lost track of Toby after and only heard later when he and Frank reconnected that Toby did get to Southeast Asia. However, the army, in its infinite wisdom decided Toby best served his country as a G2 in intelligence. So he saw few heroics 'in-the-shit', but lots of after-action reports.

Will followed Toby into school sports where he did exceptionally well, especially in football. He channeled his natural aggression and became a standout defensive lineman. He was touted as a possible recruit to the University of Illinois on a full-ride scholarship. However, grades were his undoing. He was always a C average student and even that was a chore for him. When the scholarship fell through and rather than let himself be drafted, Will joined the Coast Guard.

Frank surprised the other three with his prowess with the girls. They joked he was working his way from A to Z with every 'good' girl in the senior class, the junior class, the sophomore class and then with the fresh from college female substitute teachers. They didn't know where he found the time, but he kept at his cross-country and track and got a scholarship to Kansas University. His running had him rated among the top runners at the 1972 Olympic Trials. He was selected as first alternate to the U.S. track team at the Munich Olympics.

After graduation there was little the four shared in common. Royce was playing in covers bands doing the Midwest college circuit, playing frat houses and sororities in Madtown, Valpariso, DeKalb, Champaign-Urbana, Iowa City and Ames opening for the likes of Doug Clark and the Hot Nuts and various incarnations of The Kingsmen. He was also experimenting with pot and LSD.

With his parents on the verge of a divorce and Toby and Will in the service, while Frank was at college, Royce decided he needed to do something. So he loaded his drum kit into his van and drove out to the San Francisco Bay Area to seek his fortune and fame in the music industry. He may as well have joined the army for all the would-be drummers in the West Coast music scene. Royce sat in with a couple of groups, auditioned weekly, and was second choice for a lot of bands. He was a good time keeper, but not spectacular.

Like Toby, he kept to his word and avoided going into the army. Every time the draft board sent a letter he registered for classes at college. By the time the draft lottery was instituted Royce was a full-time student at San Francisco State College. The gigs were few and his classes were taking more and more time. There were bills and the cost of living was rising. He found he was only a handful of credits from a fine arts degree with emphasis on graphic design.

Abruptly, it became crystal clear to Royce his future wasn't as a rock'n'roll drummer. It was a Thursday night gig at the Fab Mab on Broadway in the late seventies. He was sitting in with a Flamin' Groovies type of band playing the second set before the headliners Flipper. A foursome of scruffy, acne faced, disheveled high schoolers, in what seemed thrift store castoffs, opened. Royce was appalled. None of them seemed even remotely capable of staying in tune, on tempo, singing on key or caring in the least. They would scream 'onetwothreefour' and stampede to a stop after two minutes. The crowd loved them and yelled for more. But they didn't know anymore. Then, less than thirty seconds into *Rockin' Pnuemonia*, Royce's band started to get spit at, cursed and the target of bottles and shoes. Royce, behind his kit in the back, was dodging flying shoes left and right. Even before the middle eight the crowd was shouting 'boring' and 'get off' so loudly they drowned out the band. For the safety of the band the promoter named Dirk, flanked by beefy bouncers came out and stopped them. They shielded the band from the torrent of abuse and avalanche of garbage as they hurriedly broke down their equipment and fled the stage. Out back in the alley, loading up the van, the others were pissed off, vowing next gig to go punk. Royce leaned against a green dumpster smoking. He realized music had passed him by. It was time to grow up. So sadly, he sold his drums, asked his longtime girlfriend Jessica if she wanted to get married and surrendered to adulthood. His life became a series of jobs at newspapers and magazines and finally a print company, a mortgage, two kids, two car payments and credit cards with all the trappings of being a grownup.

He heard very little of what had become of Toby, Will and Frank. He would get bits and pieces of information from music buddies in the Chicago area, but not much else. He never heard about any high school reunions, probably because no one knew his whereabouts.

Royce stopped in the middle of the old bridge into Algonquin, leaning on the buttress and gazing up the Fox River. The sun was at his back and it caught the wide river coming out of a narrow bend and widening as it flowed into Algonquin.

He glanced down and saw his shadow on the moving brown river water. Royce looked at it a long time and smiled.

It wasn't until a couple years ago that Frank had traced Royce via the internet and emailed him. Royce was overjoyed to hear from him. They jabbered like kids again, catching up. Will had become something of a mystery man. Frank thought he was still in northern Illinois, but no one knew where or how to get in contact with him. But it was Toby that Royce really wanted to know about. And, as it turned out, Frank was also in contact with Toby and it was Royce that he asked after. Frank said he would plan a get together, but something always came up. And now this-- like a lightning bolt, Toby in the hospital battling cancer.

Royce slowed down at the Algonquin Guest House parking lot, breathless.

He climbed up the short steps to the veranda and opened the door. He planned to shower and go to the hospital and see Toby.

"Mr. Partridge," Dora said from the dining room where some guests were gathered. "Did you have a good jog?"

"Yes," Royce replied. "It was a good run."

The tiny woman bustled about a table, arranging utensils as a couple stabbed cold cuts off a tray and put them on a paper plate. "We are having a little buffet for lunch if you care to join us."

"Lunch? What time is it?"

"Half past noon," Dora said.

"I don't know if I have time," Royce said. "I have to be at the..." and he hesitated. "I have to be someplace."

"Do come have something," Dora said, sounding motherly. "You did miss out on breakfast."

He had to admit he was hungry.

"Well," he said, walking to the table. "I am hungry. But only if you will forgive me for eating and rushing off."

"Oh," she waved. "That's not a problem." She again bustled around the table. "Let me introduce you. These are the Michelins, Bob and Suzette, from Wisconsin."

A middle-aged man and wife; he pear-shaped, with grey-streaked beard, she a close-cropped bottle blonde hair, gave an open handed wave to Royce. They had full mouths and were munching.

"Mr. Partridge is from New Jersey..."

Royce gave her a sidelong glance.

"Oh, that's right, silly me," Dora said with a giggle. "You are from California. Forgive me. Sometimes I don't know bees from buckshot."

Royce smiled at Dora. "How do you do," he said to the Michelins. He took up a paper plate and plucked a slice of white bread.

"The Michelins are on their way to Springfield for their annual family reunion," Dora added.

"We always spend the night with Dora here in this wonderful house when we drive down," Mrs. Michelin said. "Are you here on business or pleasure?" she asked Royce.

Royce spread mustard on the bread and unwrapped the plastic on a slice of American cheese. "Well, neither," he said distracted.

"There's not much else to life, except business or pleasure," Mr. Michelin chimed in, wiping breadcrumbs off his beard.

Royce put a slice of lunchmeat on his sandwich. "I suppose," he half-heartedly agreed, looking around the spread for pickles. "I grew up in Algonquin." That got Dora's immediate attention and an under-the-breath "oh".

"And I just learned that one of my boyhood friends is in the hospital with cancer." He put pickles on the sandwich and topped it with a second slice of bread.

"I'm sorry to hear that," Dora said. "I hope he will be okay."

"I don't know what his condition is. I came when I heard," Royce said, standing, holding the plate and taking a small bite of the sandwich.

"Would you like a pop?" Dora asked.

"No, a soda would be fine," Royce replied and then smiled as Dora looked confused. "Yes, please. Thank you." Realizing the time, Royce put down his plate, with the sandwich in one hand, and taking the offered soda, excused himself and went upstairs to his room.

The hot shower felt good. He let the water run down his face for a long time, thinking about Toby, wondering what he would find of his friend at the hospital. He was worried.

Dressed in jeans and a black and orange San Francisco Giants t-shirt, Royce checked his phone for directions to Sherman Hospital in Elgin. Sherman Hospital had one location when Royce was younger, now there were many clinics and outpatient branches. He called the main number.

"Sherman Hospital," a voice answered.

"Yes," Royce said. "I wonder if you can help me. I am here to visit a patient and don't know which of your facilities he is at."

"Is he a patient?"

Of course he's a patient, Royce thought, why the hell else would I call? He realized it was his nerves that were making him impatient.

"Yes. He has cancer. I don't see that you have a hospice or cancer ward," Royce said.

"Do you happen to know his name?"

What? Royce thought. This was like calling a computer tech support line when your computer doesn't work. Is it plugged in?

"Yes, of course I know his name," Royce was getting irritated. "Bergman, B E R G M A N. Toby Bergman."

"I can look that up in our patient index." The line went silent for a moment. "Yes, Mr. Bergman is a patient of ours. He is at Sherman Health."

The line was silent again.

"And?" Royce loudly said into the phone. "Where is that located?"

"Sherman Health is located on north Randall Road, Elgin."

"How do I get there from Algonquin?"

Now the irritation shifted to the other end of the phone call. "Take highway 31 from Algonquin to the Jane Addams, exit on North Randall Road," the voice said as if talking to someone quite stupid.

"What's Jane Addams?" he asked.

"Jane Addams Memorial Tollway?"

Royce wasn't sure, but wanted to end the call anyway. "Okay. Thank you."

"Thank you," was the curt response and quick disconnect.

Royce finished his soda, put his keys and wallet in his jean pockets, then went to the maps application on his phone. "Jane Addams?" The directions and graphic showed up. "Oh, that's the Northwest Tollway," he muttered. "That's right, I-90."

He went down the stairs and out the door without saying anything nor glancing at the people still eating and talking at the buffet.

Highway 31 was familiar, but drastically changed. It was still two lanes and winded along the northern bank of the Fox River, but along the way there an outlet mall and stores and new subdivisions. He stopped at an intersection coming into West Dundee. Thinking about seeing Toby after so many years, Royce thought about his own health over the years. He had been relatively healthy without doing anything extraordinary other than running and semi-seriously going to a gym. He did have a big scare about ten years ago when his pancreas, for no apparent reason, stopped functioning. It wasn't cancer and it wasn't life threatening. He was hospitalized for about four days where he was starved, with no food or water. That did the trick and his pancreas started producing insulin again. Idiomatic Pancreatitis the doctors had called it. And he never had a relapse. He could not stop himself, as he drove through the affluent suburban estates of West Dundee, from listing all his ailments over the years. He recalled with some embarrassment his handful of bouts with gonorrhea and crab lice in his youth. That was something never to tell another soul. He smoked cigarettes until his youngest son was born, and on that very day--quit. He realized that he didn't want to die from cigarettes and not be there for his son. He had used a variety of drugs, though never becoming addicted or overdosing. His weight was never an issue. He put on a couple of pounds, which he quickly shed when he worked out. His eating habits were neither overly health conscious nor over-the-top bad. He liked a fast food burger every so often, and chips and salsa, but not as a steady diet. He drank beer and wine moderately, and couldn't recall the last time when he was drunk. His back was strong and his knees holding up well. Royce concluded he was blessed with good genes and had been fairly healthy over the decades.

Royce merged onto I-90 toward Rockford, and was up to speed quickly. Mid-afternoon traffic was light. So Royce cruised along at 70 mph. The North Randall Road exit was but a quarter mile ahead. The toll basket at the exit required forty cents to exit. Royce struggled getting change out the right front pocket of his jeans. He didn't have forty cents, so he threw in two quarters and the bell rang and the gate opened.

Sherman Health was just across I-90 and Royce turned right onto the entrance drive. It was a sprawling and modern medical campus. The drive had a median dividing the lanes, with pine trees and tulip beds. Royce drove up to the main building, a glass and red stone building designed in a quarter round with glass entry. He parked to the left. He had no idea which building housed the cancer patients. There were people in shorts and short sleeves walking about. Some people were obviously patients being discharged. While others were medical personal, doctors in white coats and clusters of nurses. Royce went through revolving doors into the main building and stood looking about. There was a large white metal sculpture, like a tree, aptly named The Tree of Life. An atrium was to his right, and gift shops were to his left, a large bright lobby with skylights above was before him, but for the life of him he couldn't locate an information desk. He wandered the lobby looking around and finally asked someone if there was an information desk. They pointed to a dark nook on a far wall and Royce went across the lobby.

A white-haired older woman was busy at a computer. She was thin with a long face and narrow features and quite attractive at first glance.

"May I help you?" She asked as Royce approached.

"Yes," Royce said, now noticing her green eyes. "I am here to see a patient."

She turned to the computer, with hands to the keyboard. Royce spotted a diamond ring with austere silver setting and band on her left hand. "Name?"

"Bergman," Royce said.

She keyed it in quickly and the screen refreshed with a form. "We have a couple of Bergmans."

"I'm sorry," Royce replied. "Toby Bergman is who I'm here to see."

The woman drummed her fingers on her pursed lips and scrolled through screens. "Yes, here he is," she said. "Toby Bergman is at our Cancer Center. Do you know where that is?"

"No, I'm sorry, I don't."

She half stood and leaned forward. There was a peek of cleavage that Royce could not help but glance at. "Go out these doors," she motioned. "Then turn right and walk down to the next building. There will be a parking lot on your left. It's the amber building." Royce realized she was close to him, close enough to smell her perfume, Opium. She smiled. He smiled back.

"Th-thank you," he said. "Thank you very much."

"You are very welcome," she responded slowly sitting back down.

Twisting his wedding band as he went out, Royce turned and walked to the building. It didn't look amber to him. It was squat and flat with a brownish stucco and beige trim. A non-descript modern building that could've passed for a bank, boutique or wine bar.

Automatic doors hissed and parted as Royce walked in without breaking stride. The white tile lobby was quiet and cool, with light coming in from large tinted windows to the side. It had that new hospital smell. There was a center desk next to double doors. No one was at the desk so he just walked in through the doors.

The floor was very hushed. A muted loudspeaker played soothing unrecognizable, generic string music. A lone nurse sat at station.

"Bergman?" Royce asked almost in a whisper, startling the black nurse from something interesting on her computer. She had a young face, with round cheeks, large brown eyes and ready smile.

"Oh, hello," she quickly said. "Are you family?"

"No, I am not," Royce replied, wondering if he would be barred from seeing Toby because he wasn't. "I'm an old friend and I've come a long way to see him."

"Well, I guess it would be okay," she said. "He's just down to the end of the hall. Room 175," she added.

Royce murmured thanks and went down the wide white hallway. He looked into the rooms as he passed. There were patients lying in bed staring out the doorway to the hallway. They had vacant eyes and blank expressions, looking at whoever passed. Royce wondered if it was death they watched for and waited on. It gave him a chill.

He hesitated outside room 175, peering in. Someone he did not recognize lay on the bed, dwarfed by the large bed, pillow and bed clothes and surrounded by machines and screens. Slowly and quietly, Royce stepped into the room.

Now he could see it was indeed Toby, sleeping, strung up with tubes and wires. The curtains were open and sunlight shone throughout the room. Royce stood at the foot of the bed. Toby's breath was raspy and labored. He had clear tubes over his ears and into his nose, softly hissing from an oxygen tank.

Toby's hair looked like tangles of white thread, with bald patches on his freckled scalp. His skin seemed waxy, slack and almost a translucent white. Blue veins were drawn like blood highways along the limp flesh of his arms. A heart monitor beeped a steady tempo.

Royce didn't want to wake him.

There was an array of bottles and stainless steel bowls on a bedside tray. Pictures in frames of smiling groups of people were facing toward Toby on the bed. A glass vase with brown water holding dried up drooping flowers was next to a bed pan.

"Mr. Bergman!" the black nurse said loudly striding into the room. "Time for your medication," she added. She looked to Royce and in a lower tone asked, "Was he awake?"

"No," Royce said, clearing his throat.

The nurse roughly pulled and smoothed the bedding, saying in her loud voice. "Someone's here to see you."

Slowly, and with great effort Toby roused himself. He opened his eyes and Royce was alarmed at how blue they shone. Toby turned and as if blinking out of darkness, looked at Royce with his mouth agape.

"He can't talk anymore," the nurse said under her breath as she whisked around to the other side of the bed.

Toby looked at Royce with a mixture of surprise and disbelief.

"Toby?" Royce said quietly, not sure if he recognized him. "It's me, Royce."

Toby's mouth remained open, and his eyes grew wider with realization. His hands came up, as if reaching out.

"He has no vocal chords," the nurse added. "It's your friend...Royce?" She said louder, then softer. Royce nodded. "Your friend Royce is here to see you." She checked the IV and briskly went back to the bedside.

Toby nodded slowly. There were open sores and scabs around his lips. He had a grid tattooed on the side of his neck, with red rods sticking out.

"Do you need anything?" The nurse held up a brown bottle with a foam swab. Toby's eyes drifted over to the nurse and slowly nodded. She dipped the swab and swished it around his open mouth.

"For his pain," she said as an aside to Royce.

Toby looked back at Royce with a questioning look. That's what Royce took it to mean. He moved to the bedside.

"I was in New York on business and Frank texted me you were in the hospital." He paused, his voice caught. "It's been a long time, Toby."

A gurgling sound came out of Toby's throat, as his head nodded.

"Use your pad, Mr. Bergman," The nurse loudly said. She handed Toby a large pad and pen. There was scribbling all over the top sheet.

Toby wrote with a slack hand he seemed barely able to control. He turned the pad toward Royce. It shook in his hands.

Royce needed a moment to decipher the letters and words scrawled on the page. "Frank? How?"

"He and I have been emailing and texting each other for a couple of years," Royce explained.

"If he needs anything," the nurse whispered, patting Royce on the shoulder. "Buzz me."

"Okay," Royce said, as she walked out. He turned back to Toby. "How are you...I mean...how are you doing today?" He realized he was talking loudly, as if to someone hard of hearing.

Toby's hands went up, signally he didn't know.

"You're in pain?"

Toby nodded.

"Where's the cancer?" Royce asked.

Toby's hand circled his belly and with fingers outstretched.

"All over?" Royce said, interpreting Toby's gestures.

Then with a lax hand Toby pointed to his throat, to his belly, finally touching his head.

Royce's breath caught in the back of his throat and he shuddered as a wave of emotion swept over him.

"Ohhhh, man, Toby," he said, overcome.

Toby's hands raised, palms up.

"I'm so sorry," Royce added, taking a deep breath to stop the tears.

Toby, with his palms still upraised, tilted his head and seemed to shrug his shoulders.

They looked at each other a long moment and Toby seemed to smile. He fumbled with the pad, but got it and wrote.

"Good to see you." Royce read.

"Yes, it's really good to see you too," Royce replied as Toby wrote more.

"Where live?"

"I'm still in the Bay Area, San Francisco. We have a small house on the avenues."

Toby continued to write.

"Kids?"

"I've a boy and girl, and grandson," Royce said.

Toby nodded, then wrote.

"Then you not a 'mo?"

Royce read and chuckled. Toby soundlessly moved like laughter but with a choking sound.

"No..." Royce said. "Never a 'mo. What about you? Kids? Grandkids?"

Toby dropped the pad and held up both hands, his eyes wide.

"Ten?" Royce didn't believe it. "Ten? Really? Wow, you've been busy."

Toby nodded, then sunk back into the pillow, as if exhausted.

"I was in Algonquin today," Royce said. "And I stopped by the river for awhile. Remember when we stole canoes and tried to paddle all the way to Green Bay?"

Toby looked confused for a second, but then recalled and his face lit up. He made a motion toward his ear.

"What?" Royce asked.

Toby prodded his ear over and over.

"Oh," Royce realized. "The bug...the bug that went into my ear."

Toby's scabby mouth opened and he seemed to be silently laughing out loud.

"And you guys took me to a Vet," Royce laughed.

Toby seemed physically drained.

"You okay?"

Toby made a feeble okay sign with his fingers. His eyes fluttered and closed.

"You remember the river turned into a muddy creek, too shallow to canoe. We never made it to Green Bay." Royce paused. "I never told you this—but I knew the river didn't go all the way to Green Bay." His voice trailed off.

Toby's eyes remained closed. He seemed to have fallen asleep. Royce realized he wasn't breathing. He started to get anxious.

"Nurse?" He called out the door. "Hey nurse?"

The nurse stuck her head out a door down the hall. "Yes?" She said. "Is everything alright?"

Royce walked down the corridor to her. "He doesn't seem to be breathing," he said quickly.

"Mr. Bergman has sleep apnea," She explained, a hand on Royce's shoulder to calm him. "Well, that's not entirely true. The tumor in his brain is affecting his autonomic nerves. He goes to sleep, but doesn't automatically breath. He will after awhile."

"Okay," Royce slowly said, going back into Toby's room. He still seemed to be sleeping.

Suddenly, there was a gasp, and Toby took a breath and was wide awake looking around.

"You alright?" Royce asked.

Toby shook his head on the pillow.

"What?" Royce asked. "What do you need? You in pain?"

Toby found the pad and Royce retrieved the pen from the fold in the bed sheets. He held Toby's hand and put the pen in his grasp and placed it on the pad. With shaky, broad strokes, Toby wrote, "Piss."

"Piss?" Royce read.

He nodded and pointed to a clouded plastic container.

Royce wasn't sure what to do, holding the plastic container.

Toby motioned toward his waist. The tubes and the wires prevented him from reaching. There was an urgent plea in his eyes.

Royce then understood. "Okay." He raised the sheet as Toby struggled to turn his hips. Royce pulled up Toby's hospital gown, and, holding the bottom of the bottle, inserted Toby's penis into the large opening. He put the bed sheet over his arm.

"Alright," Royce said, looking upward and away.

The sound of Toby's pissing in the bottle was all that could be heard in the room. Royce felt the urine warm his hand holding the bottom of the bottle. Relief was apparent on Toby's face.

"Done?" Royce asked, when he no longer heard Toby pissing.

Toby slowly nodded.

He brought the warm bottle out from under the sheet. It had a smell like baby's diapers. As he put it on the bedside table Royce noticed the urine was orange, with specks of blood on top.

Toby was motioning for Royce to read what he wrote on the pad. Looking sideways, Royce read. "Always knew you were 'mo..."

Glancing up, Royce could almost see the old smile on Toby's face.

"You fucker," Royce laughed affectionately.

They conversed as much as they could between pad and Royce. Royce asked about Will and Toby wrote, "don't know."

"Who the hell are you?" A large woman with a stern voice said from the doorway.

Royce was surprised. "I'm Royce. Royce Partridge," he answered.

"Never heard of you," the woman replied waddled in. Breathlessly she dropped her purse, plastic bags and a McDonald's bag onto the chair by the window. "What are you doing in my husband's room?" She had big hair and a fleshy face with too much lipstick and rouge. She looked to be in her mid-forties, but Royce couldn't be sure because her features were drawn and seemed tired.

"I'm, I'm a friend of Toby's from Algonquin," Royce said, flustered.

Toby was motioning toward Royce and nodding.

"I'm Toby's wife and I know all his friends," She had her hands on her wide hips, staring at Royce. "He never said nothing about a friend named," she hesitated, then said with a sneer, "Royce."

"We grew up together," Royce explained. "I haven't seen him in forty years."

"You're getting him too excited," she said, coming up to his bedside. "Calm down, baby. Mama's here."

Toby settled down.

Royce backed away. "Maybe I should go."

Toby's eyes opened and he shook his head.

"Yeah, maybe you should," Toby's wife said.

"You don't have to be like that," Royce shot back.

"I'll be..." and she paused, dropping her head, as if she had heard herself. Quietly she said. "I'm sorry. This has been such a strain."

Royce gazed at her a moment, saying nothing. He looked at Toby.

"Toby?" he said, taking Toby's frail bony hand in both his hands. "It was good to see you, my friend. I will be back tomorrow."

Toby nodded, his eyes glistening.

Royce glanced at Toby's wife. "I'm the one that should apologize for barging in. This must be a terrible time for you." He left the room, walking down the corridor. "God, it must be difficult," he thought, then couldn't help thinking: "...that is really not the type of woman I ever thought Toby would marry,"

"Bye now," the nurse said with a smile as Royce passed the station.

The white doors opened and a group of people came through. There was a young couple with a little girl in the dad's arms. An older man in army camouflage fatigues was with an pudgy teenaged girl and skinny boy. Royce stepped aside. This could be Toby's family. He thought he could see a resemblance.

"Let's go see grandpa," the father was saying to the little girl.

"I don't want to," she cried. "He smells like poop."

Royce watched them crowd into Toby's room down the corridor. He stepped through the doors.

The drive back to Algonquin was somber. Royce thought about raising his mood listening to the radio. But then he wanted only quiet. Late afternoon traffic slowed the drive back. In his mind Royce kept seeing Toby, laying there like a shrunken bag of bones and then recalling him as a teen, brimming with energy and vitality. His phone buzzed on the passenger seat. He picked it up. It was Jessica. He didn't want to talk to her, nor to anyone right then.

Royce passed the turn off to the Algonquin Guest House and drove down Main Street in Algonquin to Prince Fong's Chinese Take Out. He parked in an alleyway and went in. It was a narrow little store with a couple of round tables and chairs on one wall, and on the opposite wall was a long stainless steel display case with various cooked Chinese dishes. It smelled of ginger and sounded of frying. The middle part of the display case had a short counter and cash register. Royce fell in line behind a young college-aged couple. They clung to each other while looking up at a hand painted sign with dishes, sizes and prices. Behind the counter a mid-twenties Chinese girl clad all in black, with black narrow lens glasses and spiky black hair and a neck tattoo waited patiently for the couple to decide what to order.

Rapid Cantonese Chinese was being shouted in a back room and Royce glanced over to see an older couple in the kitchen, arguing. Well, it sounded like arguing to an English speaker. It may as well have just been the pace of their normal banter.

"Do you mind if I help him first?" the Chinese girl asked the couple.

They looked at Royce a moment.

"Oh, no, go ahead," the young woman said, smiling. "We're still trying to decide."

"Thank you," Royce said, stepping forward.

"Do you know what you want?" the girl asked.

"Yes," Royce said looking up at the wall hanging menu. "I'd like a pint of sesame chicken, two spring rolls, a pint of fried rice and..." He looked over the tall display counter. "Do you have bottled beer?"

"Yes," the girl said, writing the order.

"Tsing Tao, maybe?" He asked.

"Yes," the girl looked up. "Good choice."

"Two bottles of Tsing Tao," he said.

She finished writing up the order and started filling the paper pints. She closed up a pint of sesame chicken, snapped open a white bag and put the pint in.

"Would you also put in a fork and napkin?" Royce asked. "And packets of soy sauce."

The order filled the girl rang it up on the register and Royce handed her his card.

"Credit or debit?" she asked.

"Credit," Royce said.

He signed the receipt and gathered the bag with food and beer. "Thanks again for letting me go ahead of you," he said to the young couple.

"Cool, no problem," the man said.

Royce parked in the Algonquin Guest House lot and took his food to the veranda, where he sat on a creaky high-back wicker chair with overstuffed cushion. The afternoon sun was warm on his face.

Dora was watering plants with a hose around the side of the veranda.

"Did you see your friend?" She called over the gush of water.

"Yes," Royce said.

"How was he doing?" She asked.

Royce hesitated opening the bag. "Fine," he lied, really not wanting to get into a conversation about it. He took out a Tsing Tao and twisted off the cap and drank slowly. The beer seemed to open up his throat and chill his stomach. Placing the beer bottle by his foot, he lifted out the pint of sesame chicken and ate a large forkful. Tasty, but overly salty, he wondered if they used MSG. He was hungrier than he thought, and was wolfing down the sesame chicken, alternating with bites of a spring roll dipped in soy sauce.

Eating distracted him from thinking about Toby. The view from the veranda was nothing more special than an old rail siding and road to the derelict Western Electric factory. Royce remembered this part of Algonquin, having worked a summer at Western Electric making toasters. All he recalled was that they had him driving a fork lift, cutting sheet metal, and working a punch press...at seventeen years old. One of the older guys had come up to him, threw an arm tightly around his neck and whispered, "Don't go so fast, kid. You'll mess up the piece rate." Royce had no idea what he was talking about at the time, but knew he needed to slow down.

He finished the chicken, fried rice and spring rolls, then drained the first beer and twisted the cap off the second. He settled back into the wicker chair and took out his phone. He scanned down his contacts finding Frank.

"Saw Toby," he text. "Looked bad. Yelled at by his wife." He paused a moment, should he send that? He cleared it and typed, "Met his wife. Big gal." He tapped send. Then he scrolled up to Jessica's work number and called. It rang two and three times before she picked up. "What?" She answered.

"You called earlier. I was just calling you back." Royce said, defensively.

"Oh, yeah," she replied. "How was seeing your friend?"

"Sad," Royce said, with a sigh. "He is really in bad shape. He couldn't talk but he seems to be ravaged by cancer throughout his whole body."

"I'm sorry," Jessica said.

"Yeah. Really got to me. I guess I have been pretty lucky, health wise."

"You do take care of yourself."

Royce took a swig of beer and smiled. "Yeah," he said, thinking of the irony. "I'll be back tomorrow."

They ended the call with byes, nothing else.

The evening was slowly coming on with the light softening in the sky to a deep purple and coolness to the air. Royce slowly sipped his beer and stared out into the distance. He didn't know if he was sad for Toby, or afraid for himself. People drove in and went into the house. Royce ignored them. Lightning bugs winked yellow above the lawn and June bugs buzzed in the trees. It wasn't long before the street lights came on, stars started to be visible and the inside lights of the bed and breakfast flooded the veranda with shafts of light.

Royce grabbed the bag of empty bottles and paper pints and went inside. There was a television mumbling in the sitting room. He dropped the bag in a pail in the kitchen and went up to his room. The events of the day had all but exhausted him, and the beer made him sleepy. He closed the door and fell into the bed. It wasn't long before he was asleep and didn't hear his phone buzz with a text from Frank.

His sleep was restless, waking and sitting up, looking out the window, waiting for morning.

When morning came he rose, showered and shaved, dressed, forgoing a run this morning. His flight was scheduled for midday and he wanted to stop and see Toby one more time. If Toby's wife was there he would try and be more sympathetic with her.

He went downstairs and poured himself a cup of coffee from the pot on the table, taking a doughnut and going back upstairs.

"Mr. Partridge?" Dora was at the bottom of the stairs. "I have put a receipt in your room for you."

"Mmmmm," Royce said with the doughnut in his mouth.

"I hope you enjoyed your stay?" She added.

"Yes," he replied, chewing. "It was good to see Algonquin again. The stay here was nice. Thank you."

"You are very welcome." Royce heard as he reached the top of the stairs and rounded the corner. "Do come back."

He picked up his phone and scrolled through texts from work. He'd reply later. He had a text from Frank.

"Still there? Say hi to Toby 4 me." It read.

Royce tossed the phone on the bed as he stuffed his sweaty smelly running clothes in a plastic bag and put the bag in his carry-on. He would show Frank's text to Toby when he saw him and they could reply. Toby might like that.

It didn't take Royce long to pack. He shouldered his laptop from the chair and rolled his carry-on out the room. A habit he had for all the years he had traveled—he stopped before closing the door and scanned the room to see if he had left anything. No, nothing left behind. "Funny," Royce thought, lugging the carry-on down the stairway. "I had left so much behind here before."

He put the carry-on and laptop in the car trunk, slammed it. The summer sun was hot and the day bright. Royce squinted and looked around. "Good-bye Algonquin," he muttered. "I don't think I will ever be back this way again."

The drive down highway 31 to Sherman Hospital was much easier in mid-morning. There was hardly any traffic through West Dundee.

Royce glanced at the green digital clock on the car dashboard: 10:23AM. His flight was at 2:40PM. The drive from Elgin down I-90 would take about an hour and half, with another half hour for dropping off the rental car. Check-in and security should take about 45 minutes, it being O'Hare. So he would have about an hour to be with Toby.

Royce was looking forward to seeing Toby again. Toby's condition wouldn't surprise nor sadden him this time and he was determined to talk to Toby about the old times and maybe get a couple of laughs.

He parked by the cancer center and walked in, going through the white double doors. The doors hissed open. Royce nodded to the nurse at the station and went down the corridor to Toby's room.

The room was empty, still.

Royce stepped back and looked to the side of the door-- Room 175. Bewildered, he went back in.

The electronic machines and array of diagnostic equipment had been removed. It was silent.

The IV stand was gone.

The bedside table was clear of the bottles and medicines clutter. There were no family pictures.

Sunlight streamed brightly into the room from the windows.

The bed was made with clean white sheets, starched, crisp and neatly turned down.

It seemed as if Toby had never laid there.

Confused, Royce walked to the nurse's station.

"Excuse me," he asked, leaning on the counter. "What happened to the patient that was in room 175 yesterday?"

The nurse looked up. "Oh, Mr. Bergman?" she said, adding matter-of-factly, "he died last night."

Shocked, Royce backed away from the nurse's station and as if in a daze walked out of the ward. He opened the car door and fell into the driver's seat, letting out a deep sigh. For a long while he sat blankly staring out the windshield picturing Toby from his boyhood vitality to the sick, shrunken shell of a man he saw yesterday. After awhile he collected himself, picking up his phone and scrolling through his contacts to Frank's number.

"Tobys gone," Royce typed and tapped send. "Gone," he whispered in the silence of the car.

With a shaky hand, Royce twisted the key and started the car, backing out of the parking space and driving out the parking lot. He turned left accelerating up the on ramp, merging with the flow of traffic on I-90 South toward O'Hare Airport. A seat on a plane flying west was there for him and in a few hours his life would continue as if without pause. He'd be with Jessica, in the house where echoes of his children through all their years still could be heard. Then, back to work, with all the little triumphs and errors that made up his day, suddenly so trivial.

He glanced into the rear view mirror, leaving it all behind.

ABOUT THE AUTHOR

Cort Fernald is a writer and journalist with numerous
newspaper and periodical publishing credits. Cort has a
degree in English from the University of Southern Oregon
and attended the University of Oregon for graduate work.
He currently resides in Omaha, Nebraska.

Made in the USA
Charleston, SC
21 June 2014